A WEEK IN THE WOODS

Also by ANDREW CLEMENTS
from Simon & Schuster

Novels

Illustrated Books

Andrew Clements

ALADDIN PAPERBACKS

New York   London   Toronto   Sydney

First Aladdin Paperbacks edition April 2004
Copyright © 2002 by Andrew Clements

ALADDIN PAPERBACKS
An imprint of Simon & Schuster Children's Publishing Division
1230 Avenue of the Americas, New York, NY 10020

Also available in a Simon & Schuster Books for Young Readers
hardcover edition.
Designed by Ann Sullivan
The text of this book was set in Revival.

Manufactured in the United States of America
10 12 14 16 18 20 19 17 15 13 11
The Library of Congress has cataloged the hardcover edition as follows:
Clements, Andrew.
A week in the woods / Andrew Clements.—1st ed.
p. cm.
Summary: The fifth grade's annual camping trip in the woods tests Mark's survival skills and his ability to relate to a teacher who seems out to get him.
ISBN-13: 978-0-689-82596-5 (hc.)
ISBN-10: 0-689-82596-X (hc.)
[1. Survival—Fiction. 2. Camping—Fiction. 3. Teacher-student relationships—Fiction.] I. Title.
PZ7.C59118 We 2002
[Fic]—dc21
2002003626
ISBN-13: 978-0-689-85802-4 (Aladdin pbk.)
ISBN-10: 0-689-85802-7 (Aladdin pbk.)

For my son,
Nathaniel James Clements

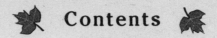 Contents

A Week in the Woods

One

Preparations

Mr. Maxwell looked at the long checklist, and then looked at the calendar, and then he shook his head. It was February thirteenth, and he was sitting at his desk in his classroom at quarter of seven on a Friday morning. And a question formed in his mind: *Why on earth do I do this year after year?* He quickly pushed that thought out of his head and turned back to the checklist.

It had become a tradition at Hardy Elementary School: Bright and early on the Monday morning of the third week in April, the whole fifth grade piled into three buses and went off for a week in the woods.

And that's what the program was called: A Week in the Woods. It was nature studies and it was environmental science and it was campfires and creative writing and storytelling and woodcraft. It was always the last big event for the fifth-graders before they went on to the middle school. It was always fun, always memorable. And the person who always made it happen was Mr. Maxwell, the fifth-grade science teacher.

The kids looked forward to A Week in the Woods. They all loved it. The fifth grade-teachers also looked forward to A Week in the Woods. But not all of them loved it. Not even most of them.

In fact, there was a rumor that if Mr. Maxwell ever moved or retired, the program might change. It might become A Day in the Woods. And at this year's early planning meeting, Mrs. Leghorn had been heard muttering, "This is Whitson, New Hampshire, for Pete's sake! *Every* week is a week in the woods!"

Mrs. Leghorn was the fifth-grade math teacher, and if she got her way, the program would become An Hour in the Woods—Without Me!

But Mr. Maxwell had originated the program, and this would be his sixteenth year as its director. As always, he wanted the fifth-graders to have an outdoors experience that they would remember all their lives. So once again, it was going to be A Week in the Woods.

Bill Maxwell was a big man. He cut and split his own firewood, and he had the shoulders and arms to prove it. He always wore dress pants and a white shirt and tie to school, and that helped make him look less rugged and a little less imposing. But it was fair to say that Mr. Maxwell had never had a discipline problem in any of his classes. Ever.

At forty-five years old, his thick brown hair was starting to turn gray, but apart from that, he looked like a man ten years younger. He wasn't handsome, but he had a pleasant face, open and honest, with clear blue eyes and a strong jawline.

He had grown up in northern New Hampshire and had majored in environmental studies at the state university. Then at the end of his junior year he took part in an Earth Day event at a grade school. That's when Bill Maxwell discovered that he loved to teach almost as much as he loved the outdoors. He shifted his major to education, and one month after graduation he landed a job in Whitson as a fifth-grade science teacher.

Bill and his college sweetheart had planned to get married, but after she graduated she took a job as an accountant for a big paper company. The marriage never happened. Young Bill Maxwell could not understand how anyone could work for an industry that did such bad things to the environment.

During his next three years of teaching Mr. Maxwell lived in a boardinghouse in the nearby town of Atlinboro. During the summers he painted houses, and he saved every penny. Then he bought forty-five acres of wooded land about fifty miles north of Whitson and built himself a log house. He installed

3

solar panels on the roof, and built a small generator system that made electricity from the stream that tumbled across his property. Before his first winter set in, he figured out how to make a catalytic converter that would reduce the pollution in the smoke from his woodstove.

Mr. Maxwell's younger sister didn't like the idea of his living all alone out in the woods. She worked for the New Hampshire Humane Society, so over the years she had made sure that her big brother always had at least one dog to share his home with.

Mr. Maxwell's mother had more specific ideas. She wanted him to get married and have some children. But whenever she told him that, Mr. Maxwell would smile and say, "Mom, remember? I've *got* children— about a hundred and fifty of 'em every year!"

And five mornings a week, nine months a year, Bill Maxwell drove the quiet country roads from his home to Hardy Elementary School so he could spend the day with his children. The drive in his old blue pickup truck took him an hour in each direction, and more in bad weather, but Mr. Maxwell wouldn't have had it any other way.

Sitting at his desk on the morning of February thirteenth, the program was still eight weeks away. Growing up, Bill Maxwell had been a Boy Scout, then an Explorer Scout, and finally, an Eagle Scout. He took his Scout motto seriously: Be Prepared. That's why Mr. Maxwell's preparations for A Week in the Woods had started back before Thanksgiving.

He had already signed up eighteen parent volunteers to help with the baggage handling, the cooking, and the chaperoning. He'd driven over to the campground at Gray's Notch State Park on a Saturday, and then tramped around in the snow to check out the newest cabins and do a careful bunk count. He'd signed a contract with a Native American man, a Penobscot storyteller who was going to give an evening performance that would include some history about the Abenaki and Pennacook tribes. He had even worked out the menu for each of the thirteen meals and the four evening snacks at the park, and had already placed the order for the food deliveries. Plus he'd taken care of about a dozen other details, not to mention writing and revising and assembling the big information packet. He'd had to have the packet ready to hand out to each fifth-grader the day after Christmas vacation, because that had become a tradition too.

True, a lot of the preparations had been completed by February thirteenth, but the checklist went on and on. So Mr. Maxwell scooted his chair up closer to his desk and got to work.

Before the morning buses arrived, he'd written a letter to the New Hampshire Fish and Wildlife

Service, replied to an e-mail from the State Park Ranger Service, and laid out the schedule of events for day three of A Week in the Woods.

As his homeroom kids began streaming through the doorway, Mr. Maxwell made three more neat little marks on his checklist, and then put it away in his file drawer until after school. It had been a productive morning.

That same Friday morning, some other preparations were just ending. About two hundred and seventy miles south and west of Whitson, New Hampshire, something was happening.

It was something that was going to have an impact on this year's Week in the Woods, but it wasn't on Mr. Maxwell's long checklist. There was no way for him to be prepared, not for this. Mr. Maxwell had no idea what kind of trouble was coming his way.

But it was. Trouble was definitely headed north.

Two

Leaving

Mark Robert Chelmsley watched from a third-floor window as Leon and Anya packed the last few boxes into the trunk of the long black car.

This is so stupid, he thought. *It's not like we're really moving. We're just . . . leaving.*

Which was true.

The large brick house in Scarsdale, New York, hadn't been sold. Everything was staying just as it was—all the furnishings, all the electronics and appliances, even the china and the silverware—all staying put. Mark's parents had decided it would be good to have a place so close to New York City, so they were going to keep the house.

And the new house? Simple. The new house was already remodeled and redecorated and completely furnished—everything brand, spanking new. Except for the antiques.

"This move? There'll be nothing to it!" That's what Mark's mom had said.

And his dad had nodded and said, "Piece of cake!"

Easy for them to say, thought Mark. *They're not even here.*

Which was also true.

Mark's parents, Robert and Eloise Chelmsley, were running a stockholders meeting in San Francisco.

"Friday, February thirteenth," his dad had said with a shrug. "We promised we'd be there, and there's nothing we can do about it, Mark."

It wasn't that Robert Chelmsley didn't care about his son's feelings, because he did. He cared deeply. He could see Mark was upset. But he also thought Mark was old enough now to understand that business is business and a promise is a promise. Plus he had the nagging fear that Mark wasn't learning to be tough enough to handle the enormous wealth and responsibility he would inherit one day.

With another shrug he said, "These schedules get set a full year in advance, Mark. One shot deal. And the people who own sixty-five percent of the company *have* to be there. And that's your mom and me."

That's why Leon and Anya had been left in charge of the move.

Mark's mom always told everyone that Leon was their handyman, and she said that Anya was her house-keeper. Mark knew better. Leon and Anya were babysitters. For him. The Russian couple had been hired five years ago, and since then his parents had been free to travel as much as they needed to, which was almost all the time.

Once it was clear there was nothing he could do to stop the move, Mark had declared that he wanted to take everything. All his stuff. He didn't want a new room in a new house. He wanted things to be the same. Same bed, same desk, same bookcases and curtains and carpets. Everything.

Mark's dad had shouted, "That's ridiculous!"

But his mom had patted her husband's arm and said to Mark, "Dear, I don't think that'll be a problem. That'll be just fine." Then to her husband she said, "Don't you think that'll be all right, Robert?"

Nodding slowly and smiling ruefully, Mark's dad said, "Sure. Didn't mean to yell about it. Whatever's going to make everyone comfortable is fine with me."

So Mark had spent his last week in Scarsdale sleeping in one of the third-floor guest suites, and a team of professional movers had disassembled Mark's room. They took everything.

And now that it was time to actually leave, all Mark and Anya and Leon needed to take were two computers, four or five boxes of food, and some clothes.

Anya called from the front hallway. "Mark? Please come down now. It's time to go."

Mark called back, "In a second." But he didn't move.

Mark's face felt hot and he swallowed to fight the lumpy feeling in his throat. He had lived here for almost three years, and he'd made a couple of good friends at Lawton Country Day School. He'd grown a couple of inches and had added some muscle to his wiry frame. Now he was leaving, right in the middle of fifth grade. Next year he'd have probably made it on to the sixth-grade lacrosse team. Maybe the soccer team, too.

Except it had already been decided that he would finish out fifth grade at a public school near the new house. In New Hampshire. And then next year he was going to start sixth grade at Runyon Academy. In New Hampshire.

Might as well be on the moon, thought Mark.

Mark had been over all this before. Like, why move now, in the middle of February, with less than half of fifth grade left?

His dad had said, "Simple. I just bought a company up there near Lebanon, and I want to get the family moved in before the end of the first quarter. There'll be some nice tax breaks if we establish residency in New Hampshire."

His mom had quickly said, "It's not that, sweetheart. You'll have just gotten back from the February vacation, and we've arranged to have the new house

10

ready then, and February's going to be the most convenient time for everyone, that's all. You can make a nice, clean break with your old school, and it'll give you a chance to settle into the area before you go off to summer camp."

Settle into the area? thought Mark. *Right, like some hick village is going to be my home sweet home. Once I start at Runyon Academy, I won't even be there for more than a couple weeks a year!*

Mark had already checked the map by then. The new house was more than sixty miles north of Runyon Academy, much too far for driving to school and back every day. So from sixth grade on, Mark would have to be a boarding student. That had already been decided too.

"It'll be good for you, Mark—I know it was good for me. It'll help toughen you up a little." That's what his dad had said about boarding school.

There hadn't been any discussion about that. Or about anything. Not with him. Because when it came to Mark Robert Chelmsley and his future, things weren't discussed. They were decided.

It was Leon calling him this time. "Mark? Come. Please. Snow is starting, and it's a long way. It is time now."

Mark didn't answer. *He* had no reason to hurry. He walked slowly down the front staircase to the second floor and into his empty room.

Bare walls, bare hardwood floor, empty closet. He went to the window that faced the backyard and raised the shade for a last look. He pulled in a deep breath through his nose, trying to imprint the smell of this room, this house, these years, trying to burn it into his memory. They had been pretty good years, and he wanted to remember everything, exactly.

But he knew he wouldn't. In a year or so he wouldn't remember this home any better than he remembered the house in Santa Fe, or the big apartment in Paris, or the brownstone in Manhattan.

As he turned to leave, something on the floor caught his eye. It was a penny. He picked it up and looked at the date—same year he was born. He thought, *A lucky penny!* Then he laughed at himself for thinking something so stupid. *Right, because all the* lucky *kids get to leave a great school and all their friends and go live out in the middle of nowhere!* Mark pulled his arm back to toss the penny into his empty closet, then stopped.

He walked slowly around the edge of the room. He paused next to the tall iron radiator by the other window. Mark bent over, put his shoulder against the radiator, and pushed. It rocked just enough. Out loud, he said, "This'll do." His voice sounded hollow in the empty room.

He pushed again, slid the penny under the front right leg of the radiator, then let it settle back. The penny was completely hidden.

It's like a time capsule, he thought. *Proof that Mark Chelmsley lived the best three years of his life right here!*

Then Mark ran out of his room and down the front staircase. He pulled the heavy front door shut with a thump, trotted over to where Leon waited for him, and jumped into the backseat of the Mercedes.

Leon shut Mark's door then climbed in the driver's side, fastened his seatbelt, and started the engine. Anya turned around in her seat to smile at Mark, but she knew better than to say anything. She knew what it was to leave things behind.

As the car swung the wide arc of the brick driveway and then turned onto the road, Mark didn't look back.

Next stop, New Hampshire.

Three

Not the Same

Anya shook him gently. "Mark, we're here."

Mark sat up in the backseat and looked around, groggy and confused. Then he climbed out, but he didn't follow Anya toward the door on the far side of the garage. Instead, he walked to the back of the car.

He stood on the concrete just inside the garage, blinking as his eyes adjusted to the late afternoon light. Looking around, Mark thought maybe they'd driven to a different planet. The storm that had promised one inch of snow for his old home had dropped eight inches onto his new one.

His eyes followed the deep tire tracks in the new snow. The twin ribbons marked the narrow roadway that stretched across a field and into a distant stand of pines. Closer to the house, the driveway ran between two fenced pastures, and every fifteen feet or so a pair of tall sticks had been stuck into the ground on either side to help drivers when the snow got deep, like today. The snow had been plowed up high on both sides of the road, evidence of previous snowstorms.

Looking to his right, Mark saw the front of the original house. The Realtor's brochure had said the old part of the house had been finished in 1798. The new part had been finished about two weeks ago: five new bedrooms, four new bathrooms, a big family room, a full office suite, an exercise room, an indoor lap pool, and a three-car garage—plus a separate living area for Leon and Anya.

The new part of the house was almost three times larger than the original, but it didn't look that way. Except for the garage, the additions had been built onto the back of the house and extended downward along the slope of the land. The only way to see the true size of the place was to walk all the way around it.

A gust of wind swirled some powdery snow down from the roof of the garage. Mark shivered, and as if she'd seen him, Anya stuck her head out the mudroom door and called, "Too cold, Mark. Come get your coat and hat."

Mark stood staring out at the snow another minute or two, then turned and walked slowly across the polished concrete floor to the back door.

When he came into the kitchen, Anya said, "I'm going to make us a quick supper. Your coat is in the

closet there behind you. Back inside in fifteen minutes, okay?"

Mark said, "I'm not going out," and turned away
from her to look around the room.

Like the house, the kitchen was part old and part
new. On the old side, Leon had already built a fire.
The huge fireplace was like a little room made of stone
and mortar. Mark could have walked all the way into
it. There was even a small granite bench built into one
side of it. A heavy copper pot hung from an iron hook
above the andirons, a reminder that this fireplace had
once been the center of the kitchen.

Mark went out through a low doorway and wan-
dered through the dining room, then a study, and a
small sitting room. The ceilings were low, and the walls
were painted in deep greens and blues. There were
old-fashioned chairs and tables, with braided rugs covering the wide floorboards. All the lamps had bulbs
shaped like candle flames. Everything tilted—floors,
walls, and ceilings—and the rooms felt cramped and
dark. The small windows didn't let in much light.

Mark studied the thick shutters to the right and left
of each window. They weren't like the shutters in their
family room in Scarsdale. These shutters were solid
wood with broad iron hinges and sturdy latches. They
weren't there to look nice or to give a little privacy.
These shutters had been made to keep things out.

The old living room had another huge fireplace,

16

though not as deep as the one in the kitchen. This one was made of brick with a broad wooden mantel. Mark went to the tall cabinet built into the wall on the left side of the fireplace and pulled the door open. He'd read about this cupboard in the brochure that the real estate lady had sent to his parents.

It was a firewood bin, almost empty at the moment. Mark pushed on the back of the cupboard, and the panel swung inward, just as the brochure had said it would. In the dim light Mark could see the narrow staircase. It led up to a secret room, and people believed it had been used to shelter runaway slaves on the Underground Railroad.

Leaning forward and looking up into the gloom, Mark thought, *Plenty of time to explore tomorrow.* That was true, but Mark knew the real reason he didn't climb over the logs and go up the stairs: He didn't like to be alone in the dark. Mark pulled the panel shut, closed the cupboard door, and moved on.

The new part of the house didn't impress Mark. Sure, everything was gorgeous, every rug, every antique, every painting. Sure, everything was designed perfectly, from the octagonal sunroom to the home theater installation to the pink granite lap pool. Spacious rooms, beautiful materials, rich furnishings.

But Mark knew how easy it had been for his parents to write the big checks. He knew how easy it had been for his mom to pick the best architects and designers and decorators. And since Mark knew that, it all seemed ordinary to him.

Except for the views. Mark had no defense against the beauty of nature. The house was perched in the middle of a large upland meadow with stunning views in every direction. The architect had made sure that each oversized window was placed for maximum impact.

At the landing on the staircase leading up to the bedrooms, Mark stopped to stare into the distance. The sky was clearing from west to east, and where there had been solid gray twenty minutes ago, now streaks of pink and gold spread along the underside of the clouds. The dark pines along the ridge, the tracery of leafless birch and maple trees, the rocky outcroppings—everything stood out in sharp relief against the blazing sky. And off to the east, the White Mountains lived up to their name. Standing still, Mark drew in a deep breath as if to taste the air, and he wished he had gone outside instead.

"Suppertime!"

Mark pulled his eyes away, the spell broken. "Coming!"

Tomato soup, grilled ham and cheese, peeled carrot sticks with ranch dip, chocolate milk, and fresh apple pie with vanilla ice cream. Anya knew all Mark's favorites, and she'd made sure to have them on hand for this first meal at his new home.

Leon took a loud sip of soup from a mug, then wiped at his moustache with a napkin. "So," he said, "what do you think of the place? Pretty great, eh?"

Mark shrugged. "Yeah."

Leon hadn't kept it a secret that he loved the whole idea of moving north. Mark's father had sent him up to the new house twice in the past month. Leon needed to learn all about the water system, the backup electrical generator, and the security system. The house even had its own water tower and sprinkler system because the nearest fire department was over ten miles away.

Leon gestured over his shoulder. "The mountains, you saw them?"

Mark nodded. "Uh-huh."

Leon winked at Anya. "The White Mountains are not so nice as the Ural Mountains, but they'll do, don't you think? But I am not happy about the soil here. Bad. Very bad. "

Mark took another bite of his sandwich. He didn't know that much about Leon and Anya, but he knew they had lived in central Russia before coming to America. Anya had taught at a nursery school and Leon had worked on a potato farm. In Scarsdale Leon had taken over part of the side yard and planted a garden. From June to October he and Anya had enjoyed a steady harvest of homegrown vegetables.

After supper Leon smiled at Mark and said,

"Come. I'll show you our new apartment."

Through a door at the rear of the kitchen, a short stairway went down to a small living room with two easy chairs, a couch, and a pair of end tables. Nothing fancy, but comfortable and homey. Leon pointed to his pride and joy, his big-screen TV. "See? One hundred and twelve channels now. Satellite. Very clear."

Mark nodded. "Great."

There was a small kitchen off the living room with a simple wooden table and two chairs. There was a bathroom, a roomy bedroom, and like the rest of the addition, everything was fresh and new. The views from these windows were not as broad as the ones from the upper levels, but the scenery was just as dramatic. The sunset was past now, and it was dark enough to see a few faint stars above the snowy hilltops to the east.

Anya came down the stairs and Leon went to meet her, putting out his hand and bowing like a fancy gentleman. "Welcome to your castle, my lady."

Anya smiled shyly and said, "Don't be foolish, Leon."

Mark felt awkward, like a stranger in their home. He said, "I'm pretty tired."

He turned and trotted up the stairs, and he didn't answer when they both called good night after him.

Mark found his room. They had done what he'd told them to. Same bed, same bedspread and drapes.

Same carpets and bookcases, same desk and dresser. And he could tell Anya had tried to arrange his stuff just like it had been last week.

But it wasn't the same. Nothing was the same.

Mark lay down on his bed. He didn't even take off his shoes. He pulled his old down comforter up around his chin and lay still, staring at the perfectly smooth ceiling in his new room.

An hour or so later his eyes closed and he fell asleep with the lights on.

Four

Attitudes

For the first two days Mr. Maxwell had given the new boy the benefit of the doubt. Maybe the kid just felt shy, or homesick. Or maybe he was trying to prove himself, be sort of tough. He was a good-looking kid, maybe a soccer player, or at least that kind of build. Sharp brown eyes, seemed plenty bright. And he certainly dressed nicely, and wore his hair neat and not too long.

But after twenty-two years in the classroom, Mr. Maxwell could spot a slacker a mile away. And by Wednesday afternoon at the end of his third class with Mark, he'd reached his decision: This new boy was a slacker.

It was written all over him. Like the way he chose to sit at the rear of the room. Or the way he leaned back with his chin up, his head tilted a little to one side, his eyes half closed. The boy didn't pay attention, didn't even pretend to. This one had a bad attitude. Everything about this kid said, "I don't care, and I don't care if you know I don't care."

Then on Thursday morning Mr. Maxwell learned who the new kid was.

He was talking to Mrs. Stearns, the reading teacher. "That new boy named Mark?" he asked. "What's he like in your class? He's not doing a thing for me."

Mrs. Stearns opened her eyes wide. "You mean you haven't heard who he *is*?"

Mr. Maxwell shook his head. He didn't spend much time in the teacher's room, so he was always behind on school gossip.

Mrs. Stearns leaned forward and lowered her voice. "He's the boy from the family who fixed up the Fawcett farm. And he's an only child, too."

Like everyone else who had heard this news, Mr. Maxwell's eyebrows went up. He said, "Oh, really? The Fawcett place, eh?"

Everyone in Whitson knew about the Fawcett place. For months they had been talking about it, waiting to see what kind of people had bought the old farm property—plus another four hundred acres surrounding it on the crest of Reed's Hill. The buyers had closed the deal in late September, and according to Beth Keene at Mountain Real Estate, the total sale

23

price for the old farm and the surrounding parcels of land had been two and a half million dollars. That was big news in Whitson.

But the news didn't stop there. Three days after the deal was settled, a building contractor and an architect from New York had come to town and set up an office in a little storefront on Main Street. The contractor put out the word that he was looking for first-rate tradespeople, as many as he could find.

High-paying construction work was always scarce during the fall and winter months, so plenty of people came looking—carpenters, brick layers, stonemasons, plumbers, heating and air-conditioning engineers, cabinetmakers, electricians, painters, wallpaper hangers, and a host of others. And everyone who was hired had to agree to one condition: All the work had to be finished by February first. The contractor was offering top wages and plenty of overtime, so people signed on and went right to work.

One team began restoring and remodeling the original farmhouse. An even larger group began building a new addition that was almost triple the size of the original house.

At one point more than sixty men and women were hard at work out at the Fawcett place. The tight deadlines meant that crews were working day and night. Near the end, some of the workers from distant towns even parked their RVs in the pasture in front of the house and lived on the site until the job was finished.

And the job did get finished. By comparing notes, the local people figured out that the materials and labor for the work must have cost the owners at least another million dollars—not to mention the new furnishings.

There's nothing that attracts quite as much attention as large amounts of money. So it would be fair to say that in the modest little town of Whitson, almost everyone was curious about these new neighbors. After all, any people who had a few million bucks to throw around were bound to be interesting. Might be a movie star! Or even *two* movie stars!

When Mrs. Stearns told Mr. Maxwell the news, his attitude toward this new boy changed instantly. But it didn't change for the better.

Because the only kind of people Mr. Maxwell disliked more than slackers were environmentally insensitive, buy-the-whole-world rich folks.

And the only people he disliked more than rich folks were their lazy, spoiled kids.

Five

Zero Pressure

George Washington and Abraham Lincoln stared at Mark from the calendar that was thumbtacked next to the chalkboard. Mark stared back and forced his mind to work. *Friday, February 27th*, he thought. *It's Friday, February 27th. So that means I've been at this school . . . exactly ten days. Feels like ten years.*

Mark was having trouble staying awake. He propped up his head and chewed on the end of his pencil. Anything to keep his eyes open. The teacher—was it Miss Longhorn? or maybe Mrs. Lego?—whatever her name was, Mark thought she was a lousy math teacher.

In fact, the moment Mark had walked in the front door of Hardy Elementary School, he'd decided that the whole place was lousy.

Before Monday, February sixteenth, Mark had

never set foot inside a public school. He'd had third grade, fourth grade, and half of fifth at Lawton Country Day School in Scarsdale. The two years before that he'd been at the American School in Paris. Before Paris it was kindergarten at the Hames School in New York City, and before that he'd gone to a Montessori school in Santa Fe.

He glanced at the fraction problems on the chalkboard, and fought back a yawn. He thought, *I learned all that stuff ages ago.*

Mark shifted in his chair and looked out the window. More snow. For the past week, at least two inches of snow had fallen every day. And Mark was glad. The snow was like a layer of soundproofing. It made everything quiet, and quiet was something Mark had begun to appreciate.

A stretch and a yawn earned Mark a disapproving scowl from the teacher. He straightened up in his chair, but slumped down again as soon as she looked back at the chalkboard. He thought, *At least I get to sit in the back of the room at this school. So I guess that's one good thing about the place.*

Mark also liked that there were so many kids in every class. At Lawton Country Day School Mark's classes had been small, no more than twelve students, sometimes as few as five. In classes like that there was no escape, no chance to slack off. Never. But here, there were twenty-four other kids. Zero pressure.

27

Scanning the room, Mark looked over his class-mates. He stared at the backs of their heads and tried to remember some names. But even a clear look at their faces wouldn't have helped him much. Mark could only recall the names of two kids. *Two names in ten days—that's pathetic!* Mark gave a mental shrug. *But so what? It's not like it matters.*

When Mark had arrived for his first day in the middle of February in the middle of fifth grade, he decided the place didn't need him any more than he needed it. In four months fifth grade would be over, and he'd be gone for good. And these kids? Were any of them look-ing for a new friend? Why would they be?

The way it looked to Mark, most of the kids at his new school had been together since kindergarten. Hardy Elementary School was an old school to them, and they were the old kids. And by the middle of February in the middle of fifth grade, they had them-selves pretty well sorted out into pairs and sets and groups of friends. Mark had no place in their universe, so he kept to his own little orbit.

By the middle of February in the middle of fifth grade, the old kids at the old school had also gotten themselves sorted out academically—and in just about every other way possible. They knew who the best students were and which of their friends were going to be in the accelerated math group or the low

28

English group at the middle school. And they also knew which girls and boys would probably make the basketball teams and the soccer teams, and who was the best artist in the fifth grade.

They knew these things because most of the old kids had been looking at each other and listening to each other for years. And they had been watching as the teachers looked and listened too. Suddenly all that information felt like it was important, so the old kids were getting things figured out.

By the middle of February in the middle of fifth grade, it was starting to feel like elementary school was ending. The old kids were looking ahead to sixth grade at the middle school. Big brothers and sisters had told them who the nice teachers were, and also which ones to watch out for. So the old kids had begun to talk about stuff like that at lunch and recess, and when they walked home after school with their friends.

But Mark? That kid who moved into that huge house out west of town in the middle of February? Mark didn't know a thing about this school or the kids in it. He didn't even know the name of the middle school.

After a week or two most new kids would have found someone who was halfway friendly, an old kid who didn't mind answering a lot of questions. Because most kids would have wanted to figure out what was going on.

But Mark Robert Chelmsley hadn't done that. He wasn't like most kids, and especially not like most kids in Whitson, New Hampshire. That's why the other fifth-graders left him pretty much to himself, which seemed to suit Mark just fine.

Even Jason Frazier left him alone, and Jason rarely missed a chance to bully someone. In this case Jason had made a good decision. Mark had taken private karate lessons three afternoons a week since he was six. He knew self-defense. Jason would have learned quickly that Mark Robert Chelmsley was not a boy to be bullied.

During fourth and fifth grades in Scarsdale, Mark had also had math and English tutors come to his home two afternoons a week, and a month before moving to Whitson, he had taken his private-school entrance exams. He'd done well, and that's why he was already accepted into Runyon Academy. Next year he'd be going to one of the most exclusive prep schools in America, the kind of school attended by presidents and senators and their children and grandchildren.

"Nothing but the best for you, Mark. Nothing but the best." That's what his dad had said.

A week before the move his mom had said, "Now, Mark, I want you to make the most of these few months up in Whitson. This school will be a nice little break before you get down to some serious work next year at Runyon."

That's what she'd said. What Mark had *heard* was this: "Mark, all you have to do is have a little fun and try to stay out of trouble until you leave for summer camp. Because what happens at Hardy Elementary School doesn't really count."

So Mark didn't care which teachers at the middle school were nice. He didn't care which kids were the smartest or the best soccer players. And if he found himself starting to care, or even starting to wonder about things like that, he told himself, *It's got nothing to do with me.*

Mark knew that his parents were some of the richest people in this part of New Hampshire, maybe some of the richest people in the whole country. It was something he tried not to think about, but he couldn't really forget it, not in Whitson.

Being rich at Lawton Country Day School hadn't mattered. Mark had fit in perfectly. The other kids there had worn blazers and shirts and ties and shoes just as nice as his. Kids at his old school didn't wear clothes from Wal-Mart. In fact, there wasn't a Wal-Mart within twenty miles of Scarsdale.

At Lawton Country Day the other kids had had plenty of spending money, just like he did. And after school the cars that came to collect the other children were just as expensive and new and fancy as the ones that came for him.

Here in Whitson all the other kids rode home on

the bus or drove home with their moms or dads in minivans or pickups, or cars like Jeeps and Toyotas. Mark was the only kid in town who got picked up by a driver in a big Mercedes. And after the way the kids had stared at him on his first afternoon, Mark had told Leon not to get out and hold the door open for him anymore.

Being from such a rich family didn't make Mark feel like he was any better than the other kids at Hardy Elementary School. Not better, just different. So he kept his distance. No sense pretending. Three and a half months, and he'd be gone. *It's not like Whitson's going to turn into my hometown or something*, he told himself. Mark knew that from the start. First this crummy little school, then summer camp, then Runyon Academy. Gone.

Apart from their new company over in Lebanon and him going to school at Runyon Academy, Mark knew there was another major reason his parents had bought the big old house outside Whitson. It was because his mom liked different places and new projects. At least, she liked them for a while. The three years in Scarsdale had been the longest time Mark had ever lived in one home.

Since his parents spent most of their time at meetings and conferences or entertaining business associates at the house in Palm Beach, Mark knew what would happen when he started at boarding school.

Once he got settled at Runyon, Mark knew that the house and the old barn and the four hundred acres in Whitson would stop being home. No one would even call it that. Mom and Dad would start calling it "the New Hampshire place." It would become just another place to visit for a while, like their Santa Fe place and their London place and their Palm Beach place. And now their Scarsdale place.

As math class ended the bell rang, and Mark jumped in his seat. The girl next to him giggled, just as she had on Thursday. Mark felt his face start to get hot. Ten days, and that harsh, metallic ringing still startled him. He couldn't get used to it. And he didn't want to get used to it. He didn't want to get used to anything at this school.

The math teacher began scribbling Monday's homework assignment onto the chalkboard, and kids began copying it down.

Not Mark. He pushed his chair back, picked up his backpack, and walked out into the noisy hallway. He took a left and headed for Mr. Maxwell's room. One more class, and week number two would be over. And then there would be only fourteen more.

Six

Spoiled

Mr. Maxwell had developed a set of rules during his years as a fifth-grade science teacher. These were not rules for the students. They were rules for himself.

For example, he had discovered The Five-Minute Rule: IF YOU WANT YOUR STUDENTS TO GET EXCITED ABOUT SOMETHING, NEVER TALK ABOUT IT FOR LONGER THAN FIVE MINUTES AT ONE TIME. BREAK THIS RULE, AND THE STUDENTS WILL THINK THAT YOU *AND* YOUR TOPIC ARE BORING AND STUPID.

He had also formulated his famous Lost-Homework Rule: WHEN A STUDENT CLAIMS THAT HIS OR HER HOMEWORK IS LOST, ARRANGE WITH THE STU-DENT'S PARENTS FOR AN AFTER-SCHOOL HOMEWORK SEARCH. GO WITH THE STUDENT TO WHEREVER THE ASSIGNMENT WAS LOST, AND TRY TO FIND IT.

The first student to experience The Lost-

Homework Rule was a boy named Timmy Weston. Timmy had announced that he had lost his science homework somewhere in his room at home. So Mr. Maxwell had called and gotten permission from Mrs. Weston to drive Timmy home after school and help him with his homework hunt. Even though Timmy and Mr. Maxwell looked for almost an hour, they never did find the mysteriously missing assignment.

So was The Lost-Homework Rule useless? Not at all. Mr. Maxwell had only needed to use that rule once. Timmy never lost another assignment, and neither did any other kid—in *any* of Mr. Maxwell's classes . . . *and it had been that way for twelve years!*

Every kid in town heard about what had happened to Timmy. It had become a Whitson legend. Every kid knew that if you told Mr. Maxwell that your dog ate your homework, Fido better have actually eaten it, because that teacher was nuts, and he would come to your house after school with a doggie stomach pump and help you look for it.

There was one rule that Mr. Maxwell put to good use every single week. He called it The Friday Rule, and it was very simple: BE SURE TO SAVE YOUR MOST INTERESTING MATERIAL FOR FRIDAY AFTERNOONS.

Friday, February 27th, was no exception to this rule, and when his last period fifth-graders came thundering in, Mr. Maxwell was ready for them. This afternoon they were going to have a little fun with chemistry.

Strictly speaking, chemistry wasn't part of the fifth-grade science curriculum. But the state guidelines did say that science teachers should ". . . foster a child's natural curiosity." Today Mr. Maxwell was going to do better than that. With the help of a little basic chemistry, he was to going to show his students that science could be interesting, sometimes amazing. And maybe even a little scary.

This particular Friday, Mr. Maxwell had an additional goal. Sure, he wanted to put on a good show so he could end the week on an upbeat. And, yes, if he kept everyone interested, that would take care of the usual Friday afternoon silliness.

But today what he really wanted was to hook that new boy, to get Mark Chelmsley to sit up and take notice, get the boy to feel like he was part of the class.

The kid certainly seemed like a slacker. And he acted like a spoiled rich kid, too. But Mr. Maxwell had noticed something else. A lot of the time, the boy looked sad. Two weeks, and he hadn't made even one friend. This year's fifth-graders were some of the nicest children he'd taught in a long time, so Mr. Maxwell didn't think it was their fault. Had to be Mark's fault. He was keeping himself cut off on purpose.

Mr. Maxwell liked a good challenge, and getting a kid like Mark to loosen up and get with the program, that was part of what he loved about teaching.

As the kids came in and settled down, Mr. Maxwell began laying out his safety equipment on the Wonderboard. That's what he called the small black-topped lab table he'd tossed into the back of his pickup when the regional high school got its new science equipment. The Wonderboard wasn't fancy. It didn't have a sink with running water or a shiny gas valve for a Bunsen burner. Still, when Mr. Maxwell dragged that little table to the front of the room, the kids all knew what it meant: show time!

The bell rang, and Mr. Maxwell put on his white lab coat, a gift from his sister. As he began to button it up, the room fell silent. Pausing dramatically, Mr. Maxwell swept his eyes across the audience, and then he began.

"In the late afternoon of May sixth of the year 1937, a crowd had begun to gather at the naval air station in a town called Lakehurst, New Jersey. The people and the reporters were waiting for something. They were waiting for an airship. This was not some blimp with Snoopy painted on the side. This was not a flying billboard to advertise tires or to take pictures at the Super Bowl. This was a huge, silver-gray airship that had traveled all the way across the Atlantic Ocean, all the way from Germany. It was nearly as long as three football fields, and it was taller than a fifteen-story building. Four one-thousand-horsepower engines with twenty-foot propellers pulled it forward through the air. And the name of this grand airship was the *Hindenburg*."

Mr. Maxwell paused and glanced around. Twenty-four pairs of eyes were glued to his face. One pair wasn't. Mark Chelmsley was looking out the window at the falling snow. *Still, he's listening*, thought Mr. Maxwell. *He doesn't have his head down on his desk like yesterday. He's got to be listening.*

Mr. Maxwell continued. "At seven twenty-five someone shouted, 'There it is!' And they were right. It was the *Hindenburg*, gliding in to tie up at the huge metal mooring tower. But something was wrong. In fact, several things were wrong. And I'm going to show you one of the main things that was terribly, terribly wrong that cloudy spring evening."

"First I'll need to put on these special rubber gloves, and my safety glasses, and my plastic face mask. And I'll also need to ask those of you in the first row of desks to push back at least two feet—so that you'll be out of *danger*."

The kids in the front scooted their chairs into the aisles and backed up.

From a shelf under the table Mr. Maxwell pulled out a stoppered glass bottle. Holding it up he said, "This liquid is called hydrochloric acid. This acid is not like the friendly acid that you find in a glass of orange juice. This acid is *extremely* dangerous. It will eat through metal; it will burn through cloth; it can cause blindness; and it will even burn through flesh and bone!"

The kids in front pushed their chairs back a little farther.

Mr. Maxwell put the acid bottle down on the table-top. Reaching below again, he pulled out a flask, lifted it up to eye level, and shook it. Little gray chunks rattled around inside the flask, making a sound like gravel in a soda bottle. Pointing at the flask, Mr. Maxwell said, "This flask contains small pieces of a metal with an odd name: zinc. That's Z-I-N-C. It's one of the elements from the periodic table. That means it's a pure substance, not mixed with anything else at all. It's a soft metal, and you've probably seen it before without knowing it. If you've ever seen a metal trash barrel, most of them are made from steel that's covered with a thin coat of zinc. The zinc keeps the steel from rusting. Now, watch what happens when I pour hydrochloric acid into the flask."

He lifted the stopper out of the acid bottle, and then slowly poured enough acid into the flask to cover the gray bits of zinc.

After about ten seconds, Mr. Maxwell asked, "Can anyone see what's happening?"

In the front row Jenny Rogers raised her hand, and when Mr. Maxwell nodded at her she pointed at the flask and said, "Bubbles!"

"Exactly!" boomed Mr. Maxwell. "Bubbles!"

He stoppered the acid bottle, put it away, and then reached into the pocket of his lab coat and pulled out a silver-colored balloon. The end of the balloon had been pulled around a black rubber stopper with one hole through it. Quickly Mr. Maxwell pushed the rubber stopper into the opening of the flask and then stepped back so he could observe the flask and the class at the same time.

Mark Chelmsley was still looking out the window.

As the rest of the class watched in silence, the silver balloon began to get bigger. In fifteen seconds it was the size of a grapefruit, and in thirty seconds it was as big as a soccer ball. Then Mr. Maxwell pinched the neck of the balloon shut with his thumb and index finger, and pulled the stopper out of the flask. Still pinching the balloon tightly, he pulled the rubber stopper out of the end and then tied the balloon shut. Reaching again into the pocket of his lab coat, he pulled out a long piece of string. One end of the string had a loop tied in it and the other end was tied to a half-kilogram weight. Slipping the loop over the end of the balloon, he pulled the slipknot tight and then let go. Instantly the balloon rose into the air, pulling the string into a straight white line. Mr. Maxwell placed the weight on the tabletop and stepped to one side.

"Now, back to the *Hindenburg*. The airship weighed many, many tons, but it had no rocket engines or airplane wings to keep it up in the air. How did it stay aloft? Look at this balloon and think. When you think you know, raise your hand."

By the time five seconds had passed, every kid had a hand in the air—except for one. Mark was slumped in his chair—elbow on his desk, chin propped on one palm—staring at the floor.

It was time to try the direct approach. Mr. Maxwell looked past all those waving hands and said, "Mark? Any idea how the *Hindenburg* stayed aloft?"

Mark tilted his chin up until his eyes met Mr. Maxwell's. Then he shrugged and looked away.

Mr. Maxwell smiled and said, "You must at least have an idea, Mark."

Nothing. Mark kept his face toward the window.

Mr. Maxwell didn't let up. "C'mon, Mark. Make a guess."

Mark turned and put both his hands on his desk. Looking right at Mr. Maxwell, he said, "Okay. Sure. Here's my guess. The airship stayed up because it was filled with a gas that was lighter than air. It was filled with hydrogen, same as that balloon, and you made the gas because there was a reaction between the acid and the zinc, and the bubbles were hydrogen gas. And your balloon is probably going to burn up with a big noise, because I bet that's what happened to the *Hindenburg*. I bet the hydrogen inside it blew up and a bunch of the passengers got killed."

For a second or two Mr. Maxwell didn't know how

to react. Mark had just spoiled the best part of the demonstration. Thoughts swirled through his mind and Mr. Maxwell felt his anger stir. It was so clear Mark had done it on purpose. He had given away all the secrets and ruined the big finish of the Friday show.

Still, Mark had been pushed pretty hard. *By me*, thought Mr. Maxwell. And on the good side, it was the first time the boy had said something in class. Plus, what he'd said had been exactly right—about everything.

So that's what Mr. Maxwell focused on, the good side. He decided to try to keep Mark talking.

Mr. Maxwell nodded appreciatively. "So you know about the *Hindenburg*? Where'd you learn about it?"

Mark shrugged. "School. History class, I guess—Hitler and everything."

"And do you remember how it started to burn, Mark?"

Mark shrugged and shook his head.

"Was it lightning, or maybe a careless smoker? Because you're right. Hydrogen gas is very light, but it is also very flammable. Remember how it happened, Mark?"

Another shrug and a head shake. Mark was done talking.

The other kids were getting restless, so Mr. Maxwell moved on. He got out a meter stick and taped a wooden match to one end. He talked about the *Hindenburg* trying to land at the metal mooring tower.

Then he punched the Play button on a cassette boom box, and the room was filled with the sound of the classic radio broadcast of the *Hindenburg* disaster, with the announcer wailing, "Oh, the humanity, the humanity!" as he watched burning people fall to the ground.

Mr. Maxwell lit the match and said, "To this day, no one knows what created the spark. But one thing is for certain: There was a spark!" And then he touched the burning match on the stick to the balloon, and—*boom*—it exploded in a flash of flame.

The kids paid attention pretty well, and they all liked the final burst of fire. But it didn't work like it usually did. It fell flat because everyone had already known what was going to happen. Thanks to Mark.

And did Mark watch the big finish? Mr. Maxwell looked his way as the balloon went up in flames.

At that moment Mark was looking out the window. The show was over.

Mr. Maxwell took off his white lab coat and laid it across the table. He stepped around behind his desk and yanked at the bottom of the out-of-date periodic table chart that covered part of the chalkboard, guiding it upward onto its roller. The chart had been covering the homework assignment.

Patting the chalkboard, Mr. Maxwell said, "Over the weekend I want everyone to reread chapter seventeen so we can discuss it on Monday. Then on Tuesday we'll have a quiz on photosynthesis and how plant life affects different ecosystems. You can all read until the bell rings."

Most of the kids got out their books and began reading.

Not Mark. He turned sideways in his chair so he could keep an eye on the clock. He didn't want to be surprised again by that awful bell.

Seven

Skirmish

With four minutes to go before the last bell of the day, the kids in room seven were pretending to read their science books and Mr. Maxwell was pretending to clean up the lab station.

The kids were actually fidgeting and whispering and counting down the seconds to the weekend, and Mr. Maxwell was actually processing new information about Mark Chelmsley.

He reasoned his way through the results of his experiment. What had he just learned by putting some pressure on the boy?

Well, for one thing, that slacker attitude? Had to be an act. This kid was plenty bright, maybe too bright for his own good. Maybe he should have been put into the gifted program. Probably ahead of most of the town kids, and not just in science class, either. Probably bored as well as spoiled.

And the kid had spirit, too. Got pushed into a corner and what did he do? He pushed back, that's what. Spilled the beans about the hydrogen and the *Hindenburg*. Maybe a bit of a mean streak there somewhere, too. Seemed to enjoy spoiling the show, being the know-it-all. Mean? Maybe. But maybe something else, too.

As he put the acid on a shelf in the locked storage cabinet, Mr. Maxwell remembered there was something he needed to tell Mark. He had some good news for Mark, and he was glad, because he wanted to keep after this boy, keep trying to reach him.

He had recently added a new item to the bottom of his Week in the Woods checklist: Give registration packet to Mark Chelmsley. The other fifth-graders had gotten theirs back in January. He had put a complete packet in his desk drawer two days ago, all stapled and ready with Mark's name written on it. Mr. Maxwell had been waiting for the right moment to take Mark aside and tell him a little about the program, maybe get him excited about it, and give him the information sheets. And ten seconds before the bell rang, Mr. Maxwell decided that the right moment had arrived.

A few quick strides took him to the back of the room. "Mark?"

The boy jerked his head around and flinched as Mr. Maxwell said his name. Then the bell sounded, and Mr. Maxwell saw Mark flinch again.

Speaking loudly enough to be heard above the

sudden burst of noise in the room, he said, "Mark, stay after a second, will you? I've got something you need to take home this weekend."

For a second Mark looked like he was going to bolt out of his seat and dash for the door. Then he relaxed a little, stood up slowly, and grabbed his backpack.

"Just come up to my desk," Mr. Maxwell said, leading the way. "This'll only take a minute or two."

Mark walked to the front of the room and stopped about two feet to the left of Mr. Maxwell's desk. The teacher rustled through some papers and then looked over at him with a smile.

"Have you heard the kids talking about A Week in the Woods?"

Mark looked at him blankly.

"Haven't heard a thing about it?"

Mark's face remained expressionless and he shook his head.

"Well, it's a week when the whole fifth grade goes to a state park campground together. And it's like a campout, except we spend some time each day doing science and ecology observations, and some other assignments and experiments, too. But mostly it's a lot of fun. Here," and Mr. Maxwell held out a set of stapled pages.

Mark took them and glanced down. The cover had some student artwork of cabins and trees and mountains surrounding the title of the program.

"We've been doing this here in Whitson for a lot of years now, and all the kids have a great time, and so do the teachers. Parents, too. We always need all the helpers and chaperones we can get. If your folks wanted to help out, they'd be welcome."

When he said that, Mr. Maxwell thought he saw a flash in the boy's eyes.

Mark said, "Anything else?"

"No, that's it, really. The packet has a lot of good information—a permission form you need to get signed and bring back, all the dates, things you need to bring with you, things not to bring." As he kept talking, Mark began flipping through the pages. "The school provides all the meals, there are boys' and girls' bunkhouses, and the restrooms and the shower facilities are almost as nice as home. It's really a great experience. Any questions you want to ask about any of it? I've been at this a few years, so . . ."

Mark looked up from the packet and said, "Does everyone have to go?"

"'Have to go?'" Mr. Maxwell was stunned. "Well . . . I mean . . . everyone always does. It's really a lot of fun. I'm sure you're going to have a great time, Mark."

"So everyone has to go?" Mark asked again.

Mr. Maxwell stood up quickly and his chair banged back against the chalk rail. "I guess I haven't explained it well enough, Mark. This is the best week of the whole school year. Every kid who wasn't sicker than a dog has always been dying to go." Mr. Maxwell was leaning forward and he felt like he was talking too loud and too fast, but he couldn't help it. "I mean, don't you see? It's like a whole week of playing hooky, so why wouldn't a kid want to go? But if you're going to put it that way, there *are* assignments every day, and there *are* grades for those assignments, and if you want to think of it that way, then, yes, every fifth-grade student *has* to go."

There was silence for a second, and then Mark said, "Unless he gets sick."

Mr. Maxwell clenched his jaw and glared down at Mark. "Right. Unless he gets sick."

Mark wasn't flinching now. He looked Mr. Maxwell in the eye and asked, "Anything else? That you need to give me?"

With all his heart Mr. Maxwell wanted to give this smart-faced kid a serious piece of his mind. But he managed to take a deep breath and say, "No. That's it. If you or your parents have any questions, let me know. Have a good weekend." And he turned abruptly, grabbed an eraser, and began sweeping it across the chalkboard with sharp, jerky strokes.

He heard Mark's footsteps out in the hall, but Mr. Maxwell didn't turn around. He kept on erasing. He heard the fire door clang shut. By then, the chalkboard was completely clean, but Mr. Maxwell didn't stop erasing until he'd gone over the whole thing two more times.

* * *

When Mark came out the front door of the school, the buses were just pulling away. He walked over to where Leon was parked, yanked the passenger door open, dropped his book bag onto the floorboard, climbed in, pulled the heavy door shut, and fastened his seatbelt.

Leon nodded and smiled, but didn't offer a greeting. He had learned that right after school was not a good time to chat. The door locks clicked as he put the car into gear and drove out of the school driveway.

Mark took a deep breath and settled back into the seat. Music from a dozen speakers filled the space around him. Jazz. Leon always listened to jazz after school.

Mark looked past the wipers at the falling snow. He sat forward so he could see better. There was no wind, and the snow was forming little piles on the limbs of the trees and on the telephone wires beside the road. And as he began to think about the snow building up on the hills around his house and on the roof of the barn, the school week began to melt away.

Halfway home, Mark thought, *Saturday and Sunday. Two whole days.* And he smiled to himself, his first real smile of the day.

They drove the five miles past the west edge of town. When Leon turned into the long drive, Mark was caught off guard again by the beauty of the place.

It wasn't the weathered house or the dull red barn or the dark rock walls that framed the frozen pond farther down the hillside. It wasn't the stand of pine trees along the ridge to the west, or the top of Mount Washington far to the northeast, hidden now by snow clouds, but still there. It wasn't any one thing. It was everything all together that dazzled him.

As Leon stopped the car to wait for the electric opener to lift the door, Mark jumped out, grabbed his backpack, scooted around behind the car, and dashed for the mudroom door. "Thanks for the ride, Leon!"

Leon smiled and waved, then eased the heavy car forward into the garage. He chuckled to himself, nodding. He knew the change in Mark's spirits weren't just because it was Friday afternoon.

Leon had seen it happen day after day. He looked forward to it now, like a daily miracle. Every afternoon it was as if a bitter old man came limping out of the school and crawled into the car. It was only a fifteen-minute drive, but by the time they reached home, that angry little man became a completely different person: Mark turned into a boy again.

Eight

Discoveries

Mark had already been to his room to change into his warm pants and socks. Anya caught him rushing through the kitchen, zipping up his coat. Hands on her hips, she blocked his way. "No you don't."

"Anya, I don't have time. And I'm really not hungry."

She pointed at the kitchen table. "Sit and eat. You are a growing boy, and outside it is very cold." It was the same every afternoon. She always made him eat before he went out.

So Mark sat down, popped a cookie into his mouth and took a gulp of chocolate milk. Anya turned and walked into the laundry room. Before she could come back to inspect, Mark drained the glass and stuffed the other cookies and the apple slices into his coat pocket. He tiptoed to the mudroom, pulled on his boots, grabbed his hat and gloves, and slipped out the door. He had important business in the barn.

From his very first morning at the new house, Mark had been itching to get outdoors and explore. But he'd had to wait. That first Saturday, two weeks ago, his parents had arrived about noon. His mom had planned a family weekend.

"Family weekend" was one of his mom's code phrases, and Mark knew what it meant. It meant that on Sunday night or early Monday morning, his parents would be leaving again. They would spend some quality time together over the weekend. And since Mark was sure his mom's idea of quality time didn't include tramping around out in the cold, the outdoors would have to wait until the family weekend was over.

Mark and his mom and dad had taken a drive together late Saturday afternoon. They drove through Whitson, and stopped to take a look at the school Mark would be attending. His dad had said, "Looks pretty small, don't you think?"

But his mom quickly said, "I've talked with Mrs. Gibson, the principal, and it's a fine little school. It'll be a good experience. And besides, Mark's only going to be here a few months."

There wasn't a lot to see in Whitson, so they'd headed sixteen miles east to Atlinboro. It was larger, but there wasn't that much to see there either. They drove around the old center of town, and his mom commented on the quaintness of the homes. They drove past the new mall on the outskirts of town, and his dad commented on how slow business must be during the winter. Then they drove back to the new house.

Saturday night Anya had cooked steaks on the indoor grill, and Mark and his parents ate dinner in the old dining room. Later Mark sat between his mom and dad in their new home theater. They watched a movie, and ate popcorn and Milk Duds and drank some strawberry soda.

When the movie was over, his dad yawned and said, "I've got to turn in, guys. That flight from San Francisco was a beast. You coming to bed now, Lo?"

His mom nodded, and it was her turn to yawn. "It's been a long day, but a good one. It's so quiet here. I love that, don't you Mark?"

Mark said, "I don't know yet. But I can deal with it."

"That's what I like to hear," his dad said. "I've been telling your mom to stop worrying about you. When things change, you just have to tough it out. And believe me, everything keeps changing. All your life, that's the one thing you can count on." He yawned again as he stood up. "See you tomorrow, kiddo," and he gave Mark a pat on the back as he left the room.

When they were alone, his mom said, "Mark, we're going to have to leave tomorrow afternoon. Will you be okay? I know it's a lot to get used to all at once. And I'm sorry we can't be here for your first day at the new school. But we have to be in New York, and that's that."

Mark said, "It's okay. Really. I'm glad you came . . . home."

And Mark had meant it. He was glad they cared enough to take a cross-country plane trip just to spend a little time with him. Mark knew lots of kids at Lawton Country Day School whose parents wouldn't have bothered.

While his dad slept in on Sunday morning, Mark and his mom feasted on fresh-baked Russian pastries, one of Anya's specialties. After breakfast, Mark said, "You know about the room where they say the runaway slaves hid, right? I found it. C'mon."

Together they wound their way up the narrow steps, Mark in the lead. The room was tiny, just big enough for a rope-frame bed and a small washstand. The walls were made of rough pine boards, and the only light came filtering up from the cupboard door below. Mark's mom had to duck to keep from bumping into the low-beamed ceiling.

Mark ran his hand along the rail of the bed. He whispered, "Makes you think, doesn't it?"

His mom nodded, and then they tiptoed back down the stairs.

Sunday afternoon Mark had gone along for the ride when Leon drove his parents to the regional airport.

At the gate his mom said, "We'll try to be back for next weekend, sweetheart. We love you very much. And you have a good first week at your new school, all right?"

Mark smiled and nodded, "Sure thing."

"That's my boy," and his dad tousled his hair. "See you soon, Mark."

And that was the end of the first family weekend at the new house.

Monday afternoon Mark got home from his first day at the new school, and finally got to set off into the great outdoors. After bundling up under Anya's watchful eye, he had gone out the back door of the garage and headed toward the woods that covered the steep slope to the south and east of the house. When he'd returned huffing and puffing fifteen minutes later, he was soaked up to his waist, with snow jammed up under his jacket, his face bright red.

Leon was waiting for him in the garage. He pointed at a short stool. "Shake off the snow then sit and catch your breath. Just sit. Now you know that no one can plow through the deep snow. So I will teach you to go on top of it."

Leon slipped the toes of his boots into a pair of long snowshoes made of bentwood and rawhide strips. He buckled the straps on the bindings, stood up and said, "First, you watch."

Leon shuffled out the front of the garage. He took a few quick strides beyond the snow banks to the left of the driveway until he was walking where the snow was deep and unpacked. "See? A heavy man, but he only sinks a few inches." He stopped to make sure

Mark was watching. Mark was on his feet, all eyes.

Moving again, Leon said, "Forward, always forward. Keep your legs apart, so, to keep the shoes from banging. And keep the tips up and the tails dragging, just so."

Leon came back into the garage. "Now your turn." Bending down, he laced Mark into the bindings of a smaller pair of snowshoes. "These are Anya's. I think too big for you. Still, you can learn."

And Mark did.

After losing his balance once, and after letting the toes dig in and trip him a couple of times, Mark had gotten the feel of staying centered on the webbed platforms. With Leon behind him, Mark went back past the tracks he'd left as he had floundered through the four- and five-foot snowdrifts on the east side of the house. "Look!" he shouted. "It's like I'm floating!"

When his mom called that night to ask how his first day of school had been, Mark said, "Fine, but you know what? I learned how to snowshoe today! Leon taught me! Anya's snowshoes are a little too big, but Leon said I did great!"

His mom said, "That's wonderful, dear. And school was all right? Were the teachers nice? And the children?"

"School was fine, Mom. So, can I get my own snowshoes?"

"Of course, sweetheart. If you can't find what you want in Whitson or Atlinboro, you can shop online. I'll tell Anya it's all right when I speak with her. Get all the gear you need, dear."

And that's why Mark and Leon had driven to Scottie's Sporting Goods in Atlinboro Tuesday after school. The snowshoes Mark chose weren't made of bent maple and twisted rawhide like Leon's. These were high-tech, state-of-the-art snowshoes made of ballistic nylon stretched over tempered aluminum frames. Both of Mark's snowshoes together weighed less than one of Anya's.

Mark's first seven days were spent in the woods. From after school until dusk, he tramped uphill and down, from one end of the large property to the other. On moonlit nights, looking out his bedroom window across the meadows, it gave him a good feeling to see his own tracks, crisscrossing the bluish snow.

If Mark's first week was about the woods, then his second week was about the barn. He had walked all the way around the barn several times as he'd explored the property on his snowshoes. He had been curious, but there hadn't seemed to be a way to get in. Deep snowdrifts blocked the doors on the lower level and also those on the end facing west. On the south side facing the pastures in front of the house, icicles had formed a glittering curtain, adding a thick glaze to the drifts that blocked that doorway. And on the end of the barn closest to the house, the huge double doors were snowed completely shut.

Then on the Monday of his second week, Mark felt he just had to get inside the barn and look around. He asked Leon for help, and together they'd shoveled the drifts away from a smaller entrance to the right of the main doors. Once the snow was cleared, it was easy to enter because the little door swung inward.

Mark had looked at Leon as the door creaked open. "Want to come see with me?"

Leon smiled and shook his head. "I have work in the house." Which wasn't completely true. As a boy in Russia, Leon had explored plenty of old barns. This one was Mark's.

The door opened into a room that was about ten feet wide and twelve feet long. Two small windows faced the house, each covered with spider webs, each loaded with last summer's harvest of flies and moths. Below the windows there was a narrow workbench that would have been about waist high on a grown man. Nails driven into the wall around the windows served as hangers for a pair of pliers, a bent screwdriver, a hammer with black tape on its handle, and some small coils of wire. Some nails and screws and a few old hinges were scattered across the bench. Everything was rusty.

On the wall opposite the bench was a row of twelve wooden pegs spaced about six inches apart, almost too high for Mark to reach. From one of them hung some long strips of leather—part of an old harness,

59

dark and stiff from the sweat of plow horses. And looking at the leather strips, Mark had remembered what a room like this was called: a tack room. Three rusty horseshoes were stacked on another peg. Mark stood on his tiptoes to lift one of them off. It had a nice feel in his gloved hand, heavy and solid, and he slipped it into his coat pocket.

But the best thing Mark had found on that first visit was in the corner of the room, next to the crude plank door that opened into the rest of the barn. At first he thought it was a broom handle or a piece of pipe. He picked it up and took it over to the windows for a better look.

Someone had made a walking stick from a straight young tree. It was about an inch and a half thick at the top, and tapered perfectly to about half that width at the bottom. A narrow metal ring, maybe a thin piece of pipe, had been fitted onto the bottom end of the stick to keep it from splitting or wearing away on rocky ground. The top of the stick had been rounded over and carefully smoothed, and in the light Mark could see the whittled cuts left by a knife. Six inches below the top end, the silver-gray bark had been peeled away—just enough space for a hand to grasp hold—and a series of little ridges had been cut, ringing the stick. Mark had pulled the glove off his right hand to see how the grip felt. Just right.

Opening the inner door, Mark stepped out onto

the main floor of the barn, the end of the walking stick making a satisfying thump on the worn wooden floorboards. A row of small square windowpanes above the wide doors on either end of the barn let in some light, and Mark could see fine.

Looking up, the first thing that caught Mark's eye was a long rope. It hung from the highest beam in the center of the barn, and a loop had been tied in the end that dangled a foot or so above the floor. Mark trotted over, dropped his stick, and jumping up, he grabbed hold of the rope and pulled, testing to make sure it would hold him. He didn't really doubt it, since the rope was almost as thick as the climbing rope in gym class. Running forward with the loop in one hand, he pulled the rope back as far he could and let it go. It swung out, and when it came back, Mark was ready. He grabbed hold and ran with it, then at the very last second, leaped up and clamped his legs around the big knot above the loop. The momentum swept him forward in a long slow arc, and then back and forth like a pendulum. After a few more swings, Mark had picked up his stick and moved on.

The haylofts were about fifteen feet off the floor on either side of the open central area. To Mark they looked like enormous shelves built out from the side walls. Craning his neck to see better, he thought, *Wonder how you get up there?* Immediately he saw the answer. The floor of each loft was supported by a row of massive wooden posts that were spaced about every twenty feet, and on several of the posts, boards and cross pieces had been nailed to make simple box ladders.

Twenty seconds after this discovery Mark was up one of the ladders and walking cautiously in the north hayloft, tapping ahead with his stick to be sure the boards were safe. When he got to the wall at the west end of the barn, he turned around and looked back. The inside of the barn stretched out in front of him, almost like it was a diagram on a huge piece of paper. The angled support beams marched away from him, the roof sloped gracefully from the peak, the horizontal and vertical supports met at perfect intervals—it all looked so solid, so permanent.

Glancing at the realtor's brochure back in Scarsdale, Mark hadn't known what it meant when he'd read, "Classic one-hundred-foot post-and-beam dairy barn." This was like no place Mark had ever been before. Pulling in a slow breath of air through his nose, he sifted the smells. There hadn't been a cow or a horse in the barn for over thirty years, and it had been at least that long since a real hay crop had been stored away. Still, even in the thin cold air of February, Mark caught wisps of all that past life and activity. And looking down, leaning on the old walking stick, he had felt a deep, satisfying connection to the place.

Every afternoon of his second week in New

Hampshire, Mark had returned to the barn. In the corner under the south hayloft he found a small sleigh, and next to it a stack of wooden carriage wheels. He'd found the trapdoors that the farmer had used for dropping hay down to the ground level for the cows and horses. He had also explored the maze of stalls and pens on the ground floor, noticing that the smell of the animals was definitely stronger down there.

Each day he found new things and added them to his collection in the tack room. He'd found a rusty shovel with a carved wooden handle, a pitchfork with a missing tine, a small hatchet, a wooden bucket, an assortment of bottles and jars, a short curved sickle, a coffee can full of nails, an old-fashioned grinding wheel with a foot pedal, a length of iron chain, four long wrenches, a kerosene lantern, and a foot-shaped anvil that looked like it had been used to repair shoes or boots.

During those first two weeks Mark had learned a lot. He'd learned to snowshoe, and as he explored the woods, he had learned to read animal tracks in the snow—rabbit, deer, squirrel, and several kinds of birds, mostly chickadees. He had learned to bundle up in layers against the cold and wind, and he'd learned how delicious food can taste after spending a few hours outside.

Besides his discoveries in the barn, Mark found other links with the past during those first two weeks.

In the woods up on the western ridge he'd found a stone fireplace and a heap of boards, the remains of a tumble-down cabin. And on a level place overlooking the mead-ow he had found six gravestones surrounded by a low iron fence, a small family cemetery. Digging the snow away from one of the stones, he read the name: Sarah Lynn Fawcett. The date on the headstone was 1825.

While Mark was tramping around the property or exploring out in the barn for hours and hours, without even knowing it he made his most important discovery.

All his life Mark's parents had hired people to fill up his days—nannies and tutors, teachers and coaches, trainers and counselors—good people, kind people, the very best available. Every spring, every summer, and especially every fall and winter, almost every minute had been filled with important, progressive activities.

And then in one day, the day they had moved up here, all that had stopped. Just stopped. No lessons, no tutoring, no sports, hardly any homework.

Mark couldn't have explained why he had stopped feeling mad about moving to this place, but after two weeks, he had. He couldn't have explained why he wasn't upset that his parents had gotten so busy that they wouldn't be coming back again until March twen-tieth. But he didn't mind at all. True, Mark still resented having to go to school five days a week, but he didn't feel neglected or isolated anymore.

That's because Mark had discovered time. It wasn't

just a sense of history, a sense of time past, that he had discovered. Mark had found his own sense of time—time present—and he had discovered how much this time was worth. This time was valuable. This time belonged to him. This time was like a bank account, loaded with days and hours and minutes, all his. After school and all night and all weekend, Mark could spend his time any way he wanted to.

And for the first time in his life, Mark felt rich.

On the Friday afternoon of his second week in New Hampshire, Mark felt especially rich. Riding home in the car after school, he'd gotten an idea, and the idea had grown to become a plan. Now it was time for action.

Mark hurried out to the barn along the well-packed trail to the tack room door. Walking quickly into the main room of the barn, he looked around and made some decisions. Things looked good, and he still had about two hours of daylight.

If all went according to plan, he'd be ready by dark.

Testing

Anya came to say good night.

She tucked Mark's covers around him. She patted his head and said, "If you need anything, just give a call, all right?"

Mark nodded. "Sure. And thanks, Anya."

He closed his eyes and listened to her footsteps, heard her pull the door closed. Then Mark reached over and turned off the light.

Dark, but not totally. An outside light was on, and it filtered in the windows, throwing pale patches here and there. Mark tried to close his eyes, but they seemed to spring open again by themselves. He tried to lie quietly, but he could feel his heart pounding in his chest. He sat up and looked around, his eyes adjusting to the darkness. And he smiled.

Mark smiled because he was inside a sleeping bag a

few feet away from the rope swing in the middle of the barn. And he was going to sleep in the barn all night. Alone.

When he'd gone back into the house after school to tell Leon and Anya what he wanted to do, Anya had immediately said no.

"In this cold? And with wind and more snow coming tonight? No, and no again!"

But after Leon had talked to her, she'd finally said yes.

Leon had offered to help him get set, but Mark insisted on doing it all himself. First he'd laid a blue plastic tarp over the floorboards near the rope swing, and then he put two thick cotton quilts on top of that, each folded double. After that came a thin, inflatable sleeping pad and his sleeping bag. Before he carried the sleeping bag out to the barn, he went to the kitchen to show Anya the label. It made her feel a little better: The bag was supposed to keep a camper warm even if the temperature got down to ten degrees. And tonight it was only supposed to drop down into the twenties.

Mark didn't kid himself. He'd been on overnights at summer camp, and he'd read outdoors books and some camping equipment catalogs. He knew he wasn't really camping. He had a soft mattress, a fluorescent lantern, a flashlight, a book, a thermos of hot chocolate, some Lorna Doone cookies, and two Snickers bars. Plus his pillow. And his stout walking stick close at hand. He even had a roof above him and walls all around. And Anya had made him bring a wireless phone.

Still, this was different. No one had planned it out and packed him up and then buckled him into a van with twelve other campers. No one had told him what to bring or what not to bring. And the biggest difference? He was alone. Even though Anya and Leon were only about two hundred feet away, as Mark sat there in his sleeping bag, he felt more alone than ever before.

Mark reached for the lantern and then stopped. He knew he was afraid of the dark. That felt like a weakness, and Mark wanted to be strong. One of his goals for the night was to keep the lights off. He pressed a button on the side of his wristwatch. In the pale blue glow he saw it wasn't even nine o'clock yet. *Nowhere near bedtime, especially not on a Friday night*, he thought. And he'd brought a book in case he wasn't tired. And he wasn't, not yet.

So Mark gave himself permission to turn on the lantern.

He'd gotten the book on Wednesday. During library period he'd asked the librarian if she knew any good stories about nature and being outdoors. She'd smiled and said, "Have you read *Hatchet*?"

And Mark had said yes.

"How about Jack London? Ever read any of his books?"

When Mark said he hadn't, the librarian said, "I don't have any in our collection here, but I know the town library does."

And she was right. That afternoon Leon had driven Mark to the small stone building on Main Street, and he'd gotten his library card and then checked out a collection of Jack London's short stories.

Mark turned over onto his stomach, propped himself up on his elbows and opened the book. He flipped about thirty pages, came to a story called "Diable, a Dog," and began to read. A few pages later, Mark wished he'd asked the librarian another question: These stories aren't scary, are they?

"Diable, a Dog" was about a terrible man who was cruel to a big dog that was half wolf and half husky. Whenever he felt like it, the man beat the dog with a club, and whenever it could, the dog kept trying to get back at him. These two were at war, and their hatred for each other was dark and primitive. Mark wanted to stop reading, but the suspense and the great writing drove him on.

At the end of the story, the hair on the back of his neck and on his arms was standing on end, and it wasn't from the cold.

The wind had picked up while he'd been reading, and he could hear sleet bouncing off the siding at the east end of the barn. The storm was beginning. A gust shook the window panes above the big double doors, and the beams and posts and rafters and joists of the old barn began a creaky conversation with one another.

Mark shivered. He pulled his sleeping bag up tighter around his shoulders and turned to another story. It was called "To Build a Fire."

This story had only two characters, one man and one dog. But at least they were friends, unlike the two in the first story. The dog trotted along behind the man through the Yukon wilderness as the man followed a trail back to his camp.

After about a page and a half, Mark realized there was a third character in the story: the cold. The cold was a seventy-five-degrees-below-zero killer, and it was stalking the man and the dog, waiting for the man to make a mistake. It was so cold that when the man would spit, the liquid crackled and froze in midair before it could fall to the ground.

The man was foolish. He hadn't listened to the old-timers about traveling alone, and he hadn't listened when they warned him about the extreme cold. Again Mark shivered and wished he could stop reading, but the storyteller wouldn't let him go.

Near the end, Mark read this passage, and then he read it a second time:

A certain fear of death, dull and oppressive, came to him. This fear quickly became poignant as he realized that it was no longer a mere matter of freezing his fingers and toes, or of losing his hands and feet, but that this was a matter of life and death with the chances against him. This threw him into a panic, and he turned and ran up the creek-bed along the old, dim trail. The dog joined in behind and kept up with him. He ran blindly, without intention, in fear such as he had never known in his life.

The end of the second story was not quite as gruesome as the first one had been, but when he finished it, Mark had had enough of Jack London for the night.

He was done reading, so that meant it was time to turn out the light again. Mark began an argument with himself. One part of him argued that maybe it would be all right to leave it on. After all, if he was really scared, he wouldn't be out here in the barn all alone, would he? But the other part of his mind said that the deal about tonight was simple: no lights. Tonight was about not being afraid of anything, including the dark—especially the dark.

Mark turned off the lantern. The wind was blowing much harder now, and in spite of the roof and walls, a strong draft of cold air rolled along the floor of the barn. Turning over onto his back, he scooched down farther into his bag. It was the kind of sleeping bag with a hood built into it, so he pulled on the drawstring until only his face and nose were left in the narrowed opening.

Mark felt blind. He had been staring at a white page under a bright light, so it took almost five minutes before he began to recover some night vision. Even then, there wasn't much to see. The floodlights from the house were dimmed by the grime on the small square windowpanes above the double doors, and the light was now clouded even more by the thickening snow. Mark could see the outline of the rope swing about ten feet away, see it stretch up and lose itself in the darkness far above him. He could see the outlines of the posts on either side of the center space, and overhead he could see some of the beams and the front edges of the north and south haylofts. But most of the barn was hidden in deep shadow or complete darkness.

Mark tried keeping his eyes shut. The noise of the wind was muffled by the sleeping bag. But almost immediately images from TV shows and movies came pouring into his thought. They seemed to have their own light, and he saw each so clearly. People with guns. Insane killers. Crashes and fires. Not to mention things like aliens and snakes and spiders. Awful stuff. Mark opened his eyes again, but that didn't stop the image flow. Shutting it off took him a while. It wasn't like turning off a faucet. It was more like mopping up a big spill when it's spreading across a tabletop. It took some work, but Mark made himself think about other things, look for other pictures.

With his eyes open, he focused on the plumes of water vapor that rose into the dim light every time he exhaled into the cold air. It was a little like lying back on a sunny afternoon and looking up at drifting clouds.

Mark began sifting through his life. He reached back as far as he could, looking for his very first memory. And he found it.

It was a hot afternoon in Santa Fe when he was less than two years old. He was wearing a pair of bright yellow overalls. When his mom wasn't looking, he pushed the kitchen door open and toddled out into the back courtyard and started along the hard clay path that wound toward the pool and the covered patio. Then he tripped and fell forward onto his hands and knees. The red clay was hot from the desert sun. The searing heat burned his hands and knees, and he began to scream. His mom rushed out of the house and scooped him up. At the kitchen sink she ran cool water over his hands, then hugged and rocked him until he stopped crying. Then the little boy looked at the bright red marks on the knees of his yellow overalls, burst into tears, and had to be comforted all over again.

Lying there in the dark on the drafty floor of the barn, Mark wondered why that was his earliest memory. Was it the pain from the burning hot path? Was it the colors, the red clay and the bright yellow of his overalls? Or was it the way his mom had hugged and cradled him?

And thinking of that question, Mark was suddenly homesick. Which seemed silly, to be at home and feel homesick. Except it had happened to Mark before.

Mark knew what he wanted. He wanted to see his mom's face. That's what always cured his homesickness. He wanted a hug and a good-night kiss. Mark missed his dad, too, but it wasn't the same. His dad always made him feel secure and protected, but all his life, whenever he'd had a strong feeling of home and warmth and comfort, it was his mom who'd made it happen. Home had been mostly Mom's department.

That is, until about four years ago. That's when Eloise Chelmsley had started to take on more and more business responsibilities. Home and business had fought it out, and Mark's mom thought she had done a good job of splitting her time and her thoughts in half. But really, the business world had won. And that's when Anya and Leon had been hired.

A blast of wind pulled Mark back to the present. It sounded like a giant palm had swatted the south side of the barn. Above the gale he heard a sharp crack and then a thump against the south wall. Mark could picture a sheet of icicles cracking off and knocking against the barn. He could also picture a mummy with fire in its eyes trying to break through the wall so it could

74

slouch across the floor and sink its rotting teeth into his brain. But he quickly pushed that image out his mind.

The sound of the wind steadied off at a new and higher pitch, and still lying there in the dark, Mark thought about his old school. He wondered about two of his friends, Carson and Ben. Good guys. He had thought maybe they'd write to him after he moved, or at least call. Nothing yet. Of course, without Instant Messenger he was way out of the loop. And the satellite DSL connection wouldn't be working for at least another week.

Another week.

Another week of school.

And that thought started Mark winding back through his first two weeks at Hardy Elementary School. He pictured himself walking stiffly from room to room, sitting alone at lunch, walking quickly out of the building to get into the big black car. He saw himself looking away from faces, trying not to care, always keeping his distance.

And lying alone in the dark he caught a glimpse of the truth: *I've been acting like a stuck-up jerk.*

Even in the cold Mark felt his face flush, embarrassed by this harsh view of himself. Almost immediately another truth came and saved him. Because Mark saw a way out: He could change. Maybe not completely, but he knew he could be friendlier. But what if the kids really didn't like him? Then it wouldn't be his fault, that's what. At least he'd know he tried. There was nothing to lose, so why not?

And then his thought jumped to his teachers. They weren't really so bad. He could lighten up on them a little, too. Just ease up and see what happens. Like with Mr. Maxwell. Just give the guy a chance.

The wind didn't die down, the barn didn't stop creaking and groaning, and it certainly didn't get any warmer. But Mark felt unafraid, almost peaceful. The darkness seemed softer, and the barn was his friend, his protector from the storm.

Turning onto his stomach, he loosened the draw-string, enlarged the opening of the sleeping bag, and pulled his pillow inside. He burrowed deeper into his little cave of nylon and goose down. He settled himself, and in five minutes he was sound asleep.

Ten

Trial and Error

Mark didn't forget what he'd decided in the barn on Friday night. He wasn't going to be the new kid at school anymore. He was going to be the new and improved kid.

On Monday morning he had Leon drop him at school a little early, about ten minutes before the first bell. It was a cold morning, so all the kids had to wait in the gym. Mark stood in the doorway a moment. He spotted a group of five fifth-grade boys. Putting on a friendly face, he walked over and edged his way into the circle. The conversation stopped, and everyone turned to look at him. Mark smiled and said, "Hi, guys."

Most of the kids nodded at him, and one of them mumbled, "Um, hi."

No one said anything, so Mark said, "Lots of snow this weekend."

A couple of the boys looked at each other and then at Mark. One kid smirked and said, "You figure that out yourself, or did the butler tell you?"

The others laughed or smiled, and Mark felt his face start to color. He knew this was a test, and he knew he had it coming. So he looked the wise guy right in the face and said, "Actually, I figured it out because the gardeners were up all night using the snow blowers to clear off the tennis courts. I always play a couple sets of tennis in the morning before school."

A tall, thin boy with curly brown hair opened his eyes wide and said, "Really?"

And that made the rest of the guys start laughing.

So right away Mark said to the tall kid, "Nah, I'm just kidding. We don't have any gardeners, and we don't have a tennis court. Or a butler. I was out snow-shoeing on Sunday, and I'm guessing we got eight or nine inches of new snow. More in some places. When does the stuff start to melt around here, anyway?"

And that was all it took. For the next five minutes Mark listened to all kinds of theories about how long it takes the snow to melt off, about how there could be some big snows in March, but the snowfalls never stayed long, about how snowshoeing was a drag and how snowmobiling was a blast. He felt like one of the guys. He picked up a couple of names, too. The kid who made the crack about the butler was Jason, the tall guy was Adam, and the boy who had his own Arctic Cat was Ed.

When the homeroom bell rang and they all started to scatter, Jason nodded at him and said, "See ya 'round," and Mark felt like he meant it. He felt like he would actually be able to make friends with some of these kids.

Getting to a better relationship with his teachers was another matter.

During second period when Mrs. Stearns passed out three reading comprehension exercises, instead of staring out the window like he'd done for the first two weeks, Mark sat up at his desk, got out his pen and paper, and did all the work in less than ten minutes. Then he took out his Jack London book and began to read a new story.

Mrs. Stearns saw him reading instead of working on the assignment. She walked slowly to the back of the room and then came up from behind and snatched the book away. "Why aren't you doing your work?"

Mark was startled. "I . . . I finished everything." All the kids turned to stare at him. Most of them were barely done with the first exercise.

Mrs. Stearns held out her hand. "Let me look."

Mark handed her the sheets and Mrs. Stearns flipped through them. "Hmmm," she said. "Seems you're done. But that means you should do some more. This is not a free-reading period."

Mark stiffened and said, "But I'm done. Why do I have to do more?"

Mrs. Stearns was not used to arguing with fifth-graders. "Because this is a reading *comprehension* period, not a free-reading period. You might be a good reader, but you can always improve your comprehension."

Mrs. Stearns went to a filing cabinet and pulled out four more exercises. She put the Jack London book on the corner of her desk, and then walked to Mark and handed him the sheets.

Mark took them from her, but as she walked back to her desk, he put his pen away. For the rest of the class period he stared out the window.

And that didn't seem to bother Mrs. Stearns at all. Mark didn't understand how she could get mad about him reading a book, and then not care if he just sat and looked out the window.

At the end of the period Mark went up to the teacher's desk and got his book back.

Social studies began with a class discussion about the Civil War. Mark hadn't done the reading, but the questions Mrs. Farr asked weren't very hard.

When she asked, "Where did the first battle of the Civil War take place?" a lot of kids raised their hands, and so did Mark. Seeing his hand up surprised Mrs. Farr, so she said, "Mark? Where was it?"

And he said, "Manassas, Virginia."

Mrs. Farr frowned. "No, it was somewhere else."

And right away Mark said, "Well, if you mean Fort Sumter, my history teacher said most of the books are wrong. Because Fort Sumter was where the war started, but it wasn't where the first battle happened. That's because Fort Sumter wasn't really a battle. It was mostly a bombardment of a fort out in the harbor. The first real battle was at Bull Run. Near Manassas."

Mrs. Farr looked uncomfortable. "Well . . . then I guess I should have asked, 'Where did the Civil War begin?' Because I want you all to remember that it happened at Fort Sumter in the harbor of Charleston, South Carolina. You'll need to know that for the social studies part of our statewide test."

Mrs. Farr continued to lead the discussion. Mark had his hand up for almost every question, but she didn't call on him again. After fifteen minutes or so, he stopped raising his hand.

English and math weren't much better. Mark really tried to be part of the class and pay attention. But on Friday night in the barn when he'd decided to work harder, he had forgotten that almost every class was pretty boring. He couldn't seem to help that. At his old school in Scarsdale the classes had been much smaller, so the pace had been faster. And what Mr. Maxwell had guessed was true: Mark probably should have been put into the gifted program when he moved to Hardy Elementary School.

When he got to science class, Mark made one more attempt. He sat up and paid attention. He raised his hand when he knew an answer. Mr. Maxwell seemed to look right past him, and sometimes, right through him. The class was plowing through a review of the scientific method, scientific measurements, and how to make field observations. For Mark it was pretty basic material. There just wasn't much he could get excited about. So after about twenty minutes he stopped trying to participate, stopped paying attention.

When the class ended, Mark waited until the room cleared out a little and then headed up to the front. He had something for Mr. Maxwell, and he was hoping it would put a smile on the man's face.

Mr. Maxwell was putting a scientific scale into the storage cabinet, and when he turned around and saw Mark, he said, "Yes?"

Mark held out an envelope. "Mr. Maxwell, I have the permission sheets."

Mr. Maxwell looked at him coldly and raised one eyebrow. "The permission sheets?"

Mark said, "For A Week in the Woods. They're all signed and everything."

Mr. Maxwell took the envelope and dropped it onto his desk. He paused a moment and then said, "So you're going? I thought you didn't want to." And he looked hard into Mark's eyes.

Mark shook his head. "No . . . I mean, yes, I do want to."

Mr. Maxwell didn't smile. "Fine," he said. "Glad to hear it." But that's not what his eyes said.

Mark said, "So . . . I'll see you tomorrow."

Mr. Maxwell said, "Yup." Then he picked up a rack of scale weights and turned to put them away.

When Mark had left the room, Mr. Maxwell sat down at his desk and picked up the envelope Mark had brought. He turned it over in his hands. It was a beautiful envelope with an embossed return address. The paper was thick and creamy, like a starched cotton shirt. Mr. Maxwell thought, *Good grief! Even their envelopes look rich! Some extra bleach and chemicals dumped into the rivers, and bingo—beautiful envelopes!*

Deep down Mr. Maxwell knew that Mark Chelmsley had just tried to apologize. Mr. Maxwell almost wished he could run out into the hall and catch up to the boy. He'd give him a big handshake and a friendly smile and say, "Welcome aboard, Mark!"

But Mr. Maxwell couldn't do that. He had already held a trial for this boy. Mr. Maxwell had looked at all the evidence, he had argued all sides of the case. Mr. Maxwell had reviewed the boy's general lack of interest, the *Hindenburg* incident, and especially Mark's response when he had been presented with a personal invitation to A Week in the Woods. The trial had lasted most of the weekend. Mr. Maxwell had been the lawyer, the judge, and finally, the jury.

And the verdict? Guilty. Beyond all reasonable doubt. This boy was spoiled *and* disrespectful *and* ungrateful—in the first degree!

And the sentence? "You, Mark Robert Chelmsley, shall be made to feel the cold displeasure of Mr. William Maxwell for as long as you shall attend Hardy Elementary School."

So it was too soon to be granting a pardon. No way.

Now, maybe if the kid actually came right out and said, "Listen, I'm sorry I've been acting so bratty and spoiled, and I'm sorry I've been acting like a slacker, and I'm *very* sorry I've been such a smart-mouthed moron who acted like it would be a big drag to enjoy a terrific week at the state park campground,"—then maybe the judge could agree to reopen the case.

But Mr. Maxwell knew nothing like that was going to happen anytime soon.

Mr. Maxwell tore one end off the envelope, pulled out the permission slip, glanced at it, and then tucked it away in the proper folder with all the others. Then he picked up the envelope, tore it up into tiny pieces and dropped them into his recycling bin.

There'd be no pardon for Mark Robert Chelmsley. Not even a shot at probation—at least not for a while.

Case closed.

Eleven

Spring

The boy who had told Mark that the snow would be gone by the end of March wasn't far wrong.

By the time Mark's parents came home on March tenth, there had already been a handful of days when it had gotten up into the fifties. Mark barely had a chance to show his mom and dad how well he could snowshoe.

The temperature still dropped down into the thirties or even into the twenties at night, but once the snow started to melt, it went pretty fast. A week later Mark had to hang up his snowshoes for good. Two thirds of the meadow had turned to brown grass and mud. There were still some drifts, especially in the shadows and in the woods, but all the snow had turned to icy slush.

His parents seemed to enjoy their visit in the

country, or at least that's how it looked to Mark. He was sure his mom and dad spent time in their second-floor office every day, but by the time he got home from school, their work day was pretty much over.

During the late afternoons Mark took them out walking around the property. He showed them the tumbledown cabin and the old graveyard. They both enjoyed Mark's guided tour of the barn, and neither of them could believe it when he told about how he'd slept out in the barn all alone one night. His mom seemed alarmed at this news, but his dad said, "That took some guts, son. Good for you," and he gave Mark a slap on the back.

In the evenings they mostly sat around the family room fireplace and read or watched TV together. His dad had to spend a lot of time on the phone every night talking to people in California and the Far East, and his mom got her share of evening phone calls too. Still, Mark was glad they were home. It made everything feel different, better.

At dinner one night, his dad asked, "So what are the kids like around here, Mark? You been getting along with them all right?"

Mark said, "Yeah, they're okay. I don't really hang out with them much because everybody lives closer to town. But I'm kind of friends with a couple of guys. At school, I mean."

"Are they nice boys?" his mom asked.

Mark shrugged. "Sure."

"From nice families?" she asked.

This was one of his mom's standard questions, but hearing it this time irritated Mark.

"Nice? How should I know?" he snapped. "It's not like I've ever met their moms or dads. Just like none of them have ever met either of you. Who knows? They're good kids, that's all. Nobody's tried to punch me out or anything, and nobody's got three eyes or two heads. So, I guess they're from nice families—all right?"

Mark's mom and dad exchanged glances, and then his mom changed the subject.

"Tell me about this outdoor education week, Mark," she said. "Anya showed me the information and the copy of the permission slip she signed for us. Are you looking forward to it?"

Mark nodded. "Kind of. It'll be better than sitting in classes all day. And the kids I know said their older brothers and sisters had a good time. Ought to be pretty fun."

"Remember that trip we took to Aspen two winters ago?" his dad said. "Now *that* was fun! You got so good on those skis, Mark—skied circles around your mom and me. Too bad we missed the ski season up here this year. The snow's not as good here in the East, and the peaks are kind of piddly compared to Colorado, but I've heard there're a couple good places.

We'll have to do that next year, don't you think? Be like taking a vacation in our own backyard. I like that!"

The best part about having his parents around was bedtime. Mark would never have admitted it to Jason or any of the other kids at school, but he loved it when his mom came and sat on the edge of his bed at night. Sometimes she'd take his hand while they talked for a few minutes. And it didn't matter what they talked about. When she pulled the covers up around him and bent down to kiss his cheek, it was the perfect ending for a day.

The worst part about having his parents around was how it cut into his time. Mark had learned that he liked being on his own. Leon and Anya had gotten used to having him disappear into the woods or the barn for a whole morning or a whole afternoon. His mom got worried if he was gone for more than half an hour.

Still, after they'd been home for ten days, Mark felt bad when his mom announced that they had to take a trip to Europe. They'd have to be away for three or four weeks. Mark had been expecting it, but that didn't make saying good-bye any easier.

Near the end of March the days got longer and the ground dried out some, and it began to feel more like spring. And at school the fifth-graders started counting down the days before their trip to the state park.

In science class Mr. Maxwell shifted his pre-woods

lessons up into high gear. They studied different kinds of trees, different kinds of rock formations, and the way that ice and plants and time can turn rock into soil. They studied how different plants grow at different altitudes, about the way rain and melt water collect to form springs and streams, and about the kinds of animals that live in and around the White Mountains.

And for the first time science class had Mark's full attention. Mr. Maxwell was terrific. He knew all this material by heart, but more than that, he loved it. The first week of April flew by, and every day after school Mark went home and out into the woods or up onto the ridge and saw firsthand all the things Mr. Maxwell had talked about in class.

On Friday, April third, when he got home from school, Mark sat in the kitchen for a snack. After he'd eaten an orange and some Fig Newtons, he got up to take his milk glass to the sink. Anya smiled and said, "I am so happy when you take the time for your food."

Mark said, "You're right, you know, about my needing food. I'm really growing, don't you think? And growing up, too."

Anya nodded, and Mark went on. "You know what I found the other day? I found this place up on the hill in the woods. There's a big clearing, and the ground is mostly level, and it isn't even that wet, 'cause it's mostly moss and pine needles. Isn't that great?"

Cautiously Anya said, "Sounds very nice."

"Yeah," Mark said, "and the best part is that it's a perfect place to camp out. And I really want to. Tonight."

Anya frowned. "You don't mean sleep out alone again?"

Mark nodded. "I know what I'm doing. And it's just right up that hill and into the woods a little way. It'll just be like sleeping out in the backyard."

Anya shook her head. "Absolutely not. Your mother did not like you sleeping in the barn alone, and she said to me, 'No more.' So the answer is no. Final."

Anya wouldn't give in, so Mark settled for the next best thing. He asked Leon, and they camped out together. Which actually turned out to be great, because with a grown-up along, it was okay to build a campfire.

Out in the center of the clearing Leon showed him how to scrape out a fire pit with a hatchet and then line it with small rocks and ring it with bigger ones. Then they pulled down some deadwood, mostly pine, but also some maple and oak branches.

Mark took the hatchet and started to chop at the wood, but Leon said, "I show you a better way. First you break off all the small pieces—good for kindling."

Mark watched as Leon took a pine bough about eight feet long and snapped off the smaller twigs until it was just the main branch, silvery gray and about as thick as a man's wrist.

"Then you find a big rock, like so. Now stand a little to that side and watch."

The rock stuck out of the ground about two feet. Leon stood behind it and lifted the branch over his head. He brought it down sharply so that it struck the rock about eighteen inches from the end of the branch. There was a sharp *crack*, and the end of the branch snapped off cleanly and dropped to the ground. Raising the stick, Leon hit it again, and another piece cracked and dropped. *Crack*, *crack*, *crack*, and all that was left was a short piece in Leon's hand.

"Now you try."

Mark picked out a limb, stripped off the twigs, and took a big swing. The branch bounced and stung his hands. Nothing broke off.

Leon chuckled and said, "Try it again, but this time don't hit so close to the end."

Mark quickly got the feel of the process and cracked the branch up into usable firewood. And even though his hands hurt a little, he knew it had been a lot easier than the chopping would have been.

There was no rain in the forecast, the black flies and mosquitoes hadn't begun hatching yet, so they made their beds under the open sky, Leon on one side of the fire, Mark on the other.

Anya had thought they were crazy, but the two of them had insisted that they wanted to cook their own dinner over the campfire. As the sunset faded in the west, Mark and Leon feasted on charred hot dogs and canned baked beans, washed down with lukewarm cans of Hawaiian Punch. They roasted about ten marshmallows apiece for dessert.

By the time the fire had burned down to embers, Mark was glad that Leon had come along. This was not like sleeping in the barn. The towering trees swayed and whispered in the breeze, and beyond the red glow of the coals all was darkness.

Both of them slid into their sleeping bags and for almost half an hour they talked back and forth across the dying fire. Then Leon yawned and said, "Time to sleep now. A peaceful rest to you." And with that, he turned over onto his side and pulled his cap down to cover his eyes.

As quiet settled over the campsite, Mark felt like his ears were growing. He heard every tiny sound, every little stir and rustling in the underbrush. He felt completely surrounded by nature, but it didn't feel dangerous or frightening to him. It was simply unknown. It was like a big book that had been lying open in front of him all his life, and he'd been ignoring it. Not anymore. Now Mark was determined to read the whole thing. And he knew he was only on page one, maybe page two.

Lying on his back, breathing the cool pine-soaked air, Mark looked up at the circle of sky above the clearing. He had noticed the sky every cloudless night since they had moved to New Hampshire, but noticing the sky is different from looking at it. And now Mark really looked.

As he stared upward he couldn't find any words for the way it made him feel. There was no end to these stars, and no beginning either. Beyond numbers, beyond distances, beyond ideas like "big" and "far." Mark felt as if his mind was being pulled out and up, off into the hugeness of space.

Back on earth, Mark heard a sound from the other side of the fire pit. Leon had begun to snore softly, his breathing slow and deep. The rhythm was comforting, and after a long day it was all the lullaby Mark needed.

Twelve

Gearing Up

The world of camping gear was a revelation to Mark. After the computer in the family room had been linked up to the DSL connection, Mark discovered more than a dozen terrific stores on the web that specialized in getting people ready to deal with Mother Nature. Eastern Mountain Sports, Mountain Equipment Co-Op, L.L. Bean, Sierra Outfitters—the list went on and on.

Mark's favorite was REI—Recreational Equipment Incorporated. The REI Web site was organized by activities, and each category branched off into a tantalizing selection of gadgets and tools and necessities for enjoying time in the great outdoors. Tents, sleeping bags, rock climbing gear, mountain bikes, kayaks and canoes, camping stoves, knives, communication equipment, maps and direction finders, shoes and boots of every imaginable kind, sunglasses and binoculars, and an endless assortment of different kinds of special outdoor clothing. The variety was overwhelming.

On Sunday morning when his mom called from London, Mark told her about how he had camped out with Leon Friday night. Then he said, "I really want to do a lot of overnight trips at camp this summer, maybe even do the ten-day mountain trip in Maine. I looked at the booklet from camp, and it says if you're twelve, it's all right—and I'll be twelve in June."

"Well, we can certainly talk about that, Mark," his mom said. Mark could tell she didn't like the idea. But she hadn't said no, so that was okay, and it was the perfect opening for what he really wanted to ask her.

Mark said, "Well, since I want to get into camping, I've been looking at some catalogs that have equipment and stuff. So would it be okay if I got some gear, just so I could be ready? In case I get to go on some overnights this summer?"

And just like he knew she would, his mom said, "Why, of course you may, dear. Get whatever you think you need. When I talk to Anya I'll ask her to let you use the American Express card. Just promise me you won't get anything that's dangerous, all right? No big knives . . . or axes—nothing like that, all right?"

Mark said, "Nothing like that, I promise. I just want to learn how to be a good camper, that's all."

"Well, I think that's wonderful, dear."

Late Sunday afternoon, Mark turned on the Mac. Then he opened up the browser and clicked on the REI Web site. And he realized he had a problem. His problem was that he wanted everything. And thanks to his mom's credit card, he could actually afford everything. Well, not everything, but there were still way too many choices.

Mark had to decide what he really needed. So he opened a new window in the browser, clicked on a search engine, and typed in "camping essentials." On the second page of listings, he found a web page put together by a guy from Wyoming who taught outdoor survival classes. He called himself "Mr. Survival." He had organized his list of essential gear by looking at the greatest dangers people usually face if they get lost in the wilderness.

The first danger on his list was getting too cold—or too hot. So he had a section of information about clothing layers, and choosing the right socks and footwear. Mark felt proud that he'd already figured out those things on his own. Mr. Survival also recommended carrying a plastic "space blanket." You could put the shiny side in to keep warm, or put the shiny side out to keep the sun off. It would also shed rain or snow.

Next on the danger list came thirst and hunger. He recommended carrying at least two water bottles and also having a way to purify more. Mr. Survival's personal favorite was a tiny bottle of liquid iodine drops. He wrote,

You can scoop water right out of a stream or even a puddle, add a few drops of iodine, wait ten minutes, and take a drink. It might taste bad, but you won't get sick from germs or parasites, and most importantly, you won't get weak from dehydration or die of thirst.

About hunger, he said,

Even a day-hiker should carry five or six energy bars and two or three regular candy bars. A candy bar doesn't weigh much, and it might just give you that jolt of energy you need to get yourself up out of the ravine you fell into.

The list went on:

- Take at least two ways to make fire, plus a fire starter.

  Best emergency fire maker: a magnesium block and a striker made from three inches of hacksaw blade. Direct a shower of sparks onto some scrapings from the block.

  Best fire starter: cotton balls covered with petroleum jelly—ten will stuff into one plastic film container. If you don't have this, use finely shredded birch bark, dry grass, lint from your socks, or a candy bar wrapper.
- Take a compass, and know how to use it.
- Take a small waterproof flashlight or headlamp—and extra batteries.
- Take a pocketknife.

- Take a loud whistle, like a lifeguard's whistle, to help others find you if you get lost or separated.
- Take a dozen cloth-strip Band-Aids and a small roll of duct tape for cuts or foot blisters.
- Take a small magnifying glass for map reading or starting a fire.
- Take two zip-seal plastic bags for carrying water.
- Take a roll of dental floss or other strong, light cord—at least a hundred feet—and a strong sewing needle.

After reading what Mr. Survival had to say, Mark felt ready to start shopping. He clicked back to the REI Web site, and started filling his online shopping basket.

First he picked out a new sleeping bag. The one he'd been using had been to summer camp three times. It was plenty warm, but it weighed too much. The new bag Mark picked out was filled with goose down. It weighed less than three pounds and packed up into a thin, tight roll.

The next essential item was a pack—not a simple backpack, but a framepack. Mark had used one at camp last summer. It was called a framepack because it had a built-in frame of metal or fiberglass to keep it stiff and spread out the weight of a load in the best way possible. After reading the descriptions of about ten different packs, Mark looked at a chart and picked the one that was best for a person of his height and weight.

From about twenty different kinds of flashlights, he picked a Mini-Maglite that used AA batteries. He also chose a headlamp, like a flashlight on a head strap. The one he picked had three different levels of brightness, and would run for anywhere from 12 to 150 hours on three AAA batteries.

The magnesium fire-starting bar seemed kind of silly to Mark. Why bother carrying that if you already have matches or a lighter? He flipped back to Mr. Survival's web page and clicked on the link about fire making. And Mr. Survival made it simple:

> Matches go bad or get wet, even the waterproof kind. Lighters rust or break or leak. Some magnesium scrapings and a shower of sparks from a bit of hacksaw blade will always work, no matter how long you've had them and no matter whether it's raining or snowing or ten below zero.

So Mark clicked on the magnesium fire block with the built-in striker bar and put it into his online shopping basket.

Even though Mark knew he wouldn't be allowed to use it by himself, he picked out a little gas-powered cooking stove anyway. And then he found a good compass, a pair of lightweight binoculars, and six pairs of special "moisture wicking" hiking socks. Plus a dozen chocolate chip energy bars.

He looked at the boots, but the Italian hiking boots he had gotten before camp last summer still fit perfectly, and they were all broken in, too.

When Mark went to the page that showed the knives, he remembered what his mom had made him promise. She'd said no big knives or axes. But she hadn't said he couldn't get a *smaller* knife. After all, his dad had already given him a Swiss Army knife for Christmas two years ago. So Mark picked out a light-weight knife with a black plastic handle and a single blade that locked open. Definitely not a big knife.

He could have kept finding great stuff all evening, but Mark felt like he'd better stop. He clicked on his shopping basket, and then on the "checkout" box. The total amount came to more than eleven hundred dollars!

Mark stared at the number. Eleven hundred dollars was a lot of money. He started to look at the list of things he'd chosen, trying to figure out which ones to put back.

Then Mark remembered the skis and boots and poles his dad had helped him pick out when they went to Aspen that time. Plus the jacket and goggles and gloves. Mark had used those skis for less than a week, and now all that equipment was lying in a closet back in Scarsdale, too small to ever use again. And those things had cost his dad more than nine hundred bucks.

So getting all this stuff for only eleven hundred? Suddenly that seemed like a bargain. And Mark knew he wouldn't be using these things for only a week or two, either.

He quickly filled in the shipping information, typed in his mom's credit card number, and clicked on the Buy Now button. Less than ten seconds later a confirmation screen appeared and promised that the purchased items would be delivered to his house by Federal Express on Tuesday afternoon.

Mark printed a copy of the confirmation page, closed the browser, and shut down the computer.

Then he went to the kitchen to get himself a snack. All that shopping had made him hungry.

Thirteen

Readiness

After the announcements and the Pledge of Allegiance on Monday morning, Mark was surprised when the principal's voice came crackling out of the speaker in his homeroom.

"Good morning, fifth-graders. This is Mrs. Gibson. By this time next Monday, you will already be well on your way to Gray's Notch State Park. Mr. Maxwell tells me that three of you have not yet turned in your signed permission slips for your Week in the Woods. If you are one of those three, please take care of this right away. You must turn in a signed slip or you will not be allowed to get onto the bus. The buses will leave from the front of the school building at seven-thirty next Monday morning. That means you all should be here by seven o'clock at the very latest. Your information packet is very clear about all the details.

Please read through the information with your parents again this week. And students, make sure that you don't bring too much with you. We have a problem with this every year. Each student may bring no more than one medium-sized suitcase, one book bag, and a sleeping bag. There is a very clear packing list, and if you follow it, you'll have just enough of everything. If you have any questions, ask any of your teachers or, of course, you may ask Mr. Maxwell. Have a great week, everybody."

The whole rest of the day was just as surprising to Mark. Everything was about the big trip. No school Mark had attended had ever focused on a single idea the way that Hardy Elementary School zeroed in on A Week in the Woods.

In language arts Mrs. Bender taught a lesson about keeping a journal, and then each student made a small booklet to write in during the week away. "We shall do our best to make our observations original, interesting, and accurate."

In social studies they learned about the Native Americans who had lived in the region, and on a special map Mrs. Farr showed a hilltop at the park that was off-limits to all hikers. Some Abenaki artifacts had been discovered there last year, and over the coming summer there would be a formal archeological survey of the area. Then Mrs. Farr gave each kid a folder with a topographic map of the park. She explained how to read the map, and how to use the position of the sun or even where the moss was growing on a tree to figure out which way was north. She said, "I want everyone to bring these folders with you to the park next week. On Tuesday and Wednesday afternoon, we'll be doing some trail finding and some orienteering, and I don't want any of you getting lost."

In math class Mrs. Leghorn had them do some problems about rate and distance.

"All right, class," she said. "If you walk at six miles an hour, and you hike for three hours and twenty minutes—my goodness! Why *anyone* would want to go tramping around out in the cold for that long is beyond me. But if you *did* go hiking for that long, then how many miles would you have walked? Assuming you were still alive, that is."

Mark didn't think Mrs. Leghorn was very excited about going to the woods.

In gym class Mr. Harris had turned half of the general purpose room into an obstacle course. The course involved a lot of ducking under things, a lot of climbing over things, and some careful walking across the low balance beam without falling into the fake water. He had also built a small hill out of fifteen or twenty tumbling mats and the pommel horse.

Even the music teacher put preparations for the fifth grade spring concert on hold so everyone could learn some campfire songs.

The whole fifth grade was moving toward the same goal, and of course, Mr. Maxwell was leading the charge.

When science class began on Monday afternoon, Mr. Maxwell smiled broadly and said, "This time next week, we'll all be seventy-five miles away from here, breathing in some cool mountain air. So let's talk a little bit about air quality, shall we? First of all, what is air made up of?"

A girl named Chelsea raised her hand, and Mr. Maxwell nodded at her. She said, "Oxygen? And nitrogen?"

Mr. Maxwell nodded. "Yup. Anything else? Anyone?"

No other hands went up.

Mark knew something about this because he'd done a science fair project in third grade about air pollution. So he raised his hand. His was the only hand in the air.

Mr. Maxwell looked around the room. It was impossible to miss Mark's hand.

"Anyone?" Mr. Maxwell asked again. "No? Well, air is actually made up of a number of gases, and oxygen and nitrogen are two of them, just as Chelsea said."

Mark brought his hand down, and he felt his face start to get warm. He felt like he'd been smacked on the cheek.

He wouldn't have been able to put it into words

very well, but Mark knew what was going on. He knew what this thing with Mr. Maxwell was about. And Mark felt like it was pretty much his own fault. He knew he had been unpleasant and rude to Mr. Maxwell during his first couple of weeks. Mark knew he had offended the man, especially by not getting excited about the big trip.

But Mark also knew that for his part, he'd let all that go. All of it. He wanted to be part of the class now, he wanted in. And he thought he'd been sending clear signals to Mr. Maxwell, friendly signals.

For a while Mark had thought that the science teacher wasn't getting the message. And then for a couple of weeks Mark had felt that maybe Mr. Maxwell had a right to ignore him, to keep him out in the cold, test him to be sure he was sincere.

But today Mark felt hurt. And embarrassed. Today he got the point. And the point was that Mr. Maxwell was punishing him. Mark wanted in, and Mr. Maxwell knew it, but he had just slammed the door in Mark's face.

To his credit, Mark didn't get angry. He didn't tune out the class and stare at the floor or look out the window. Instead he swallowed hard and tried to keep listening. He didn't let himself brood about the way Mr. Maxwell was treating him. He kept his mind focused on what the teacher was saying.

Because Mark truly wanted to learn about the

woods and the mountains and the air and the weather—
all of it. And whatever else he was, Mark had to admit
that Mr. Maxwell was an expert.

He just wasn't a very nice expert.

When Mark got home from school Tuesday there
were four large cardboard boxes from REI waiting for
him in the garage. Leon helped him unpack everything, whistling softly now and then in appreciation,
sometimes asking Mark to explain a piece of equipment.

"Very fancy," he said as Mark unrolled the bright
orange sleeping bag to get a better look at it. "When I
was a boy, I had an iron frying pan, a blanket roll tied
with a piece of rope, a penknife, and a small axe. That
was camping."

Mark tucked the smaller gear like the magnesium
block and the iodine drops and the flashlights right
into the outer pockets on his new framepack. He
stuffed the sleeping bag inside the pack to give it some
shape and weight, and then Leon helped him to move
and adjust the shoulder straps so that it fit on his back
correctly. Standing there with the straps fastened and
the buckles clipped, Mark imagined himself at summer camp, all set for a ten-day hike. It made him feel
strong and independent.

And at that moment Anya called from the kitchen
door, "Both of you, come inside now. Mark, change

107

your clothes and eat before you play with your new toys. Come."

Later on Mark took his new compass out into the woods. He sat on a fallen tree and read the instruction booklet from beginning to end. Then he did some of the recommended training exercises. He learned how to sight on a distant object, and he learned to count his steps so he could estimate how far he'd traveled in one direction. He didn't have a map to test it on, but he understood how to put the clear plastic base of the compass onto a map and then turn the map to line it up and get a true idea about the lay of the land.

Then Mark laid out a simple course for himself, a big triangle: first east, then northwest, then southeast. With his eyes glued to the red and black needle of the compass, Mark paced off his course. Thirty minutes later he ended up back within fifty feet of his starting point. Mark felt like he'd just sailed around the globe.

After dinner Mark carried all his new equipment up to his room. He laid it out on the floor and on his bed. Then he got his Week in the Woods packet and found the packing list. Item by item, Mark laid out what he needed to take. Then he refolded all his clothes. Carefully he laid his belongings into his new pack. It all fit in easily, even his hiking boots.

Mark took another look at the packing list, and in the section about what not to bring he saw, "No knives of any kind." So he dug into the outside pocket of his backpack, found his new knife and walked across the room and dropped it into his desk drawer. The list also said, "No matches or lighters." But it didn't say no magnesium striker blocks, so Mark left that in his backpack pocket.

Then Mark sat at his desk and made a list of things he still needed, especially things that Mr. Survival said he ought to have.

He still needed a space blanket, a piece of hacksaw blade, two zip-seal plastic bags, some candy bars, a whistle, Band-Aids, some duct tape, some extra batteries, a magnifying glass, and some dental floss. And a heavy-duty sewing needle. The things he couldn't find around the house he'd get at Wal-Mart, and Leon could take him there after school tomorrow or the next day.

Mark pushed his new sleeping bag into its stuff sack—a waterproof nylon bag with a drawstring at the open end. There were special straps on the bottom of his framepack, and after a little fiddling Mark got the bag fastened into position.

Then came the moment of truth. Mark took hold of the pack and swung it around and up onto his back. He slipped the shoulder bands into place, fastened the chest strap, settled the waist belt onto his hips and then pulled it tight and snapped the buckle. Taking a few strides around his room, he tested the weight. Felt like about twenty-five pounds. Not too bad. Very doable.

And again Mark had that feeling of strength and independence. Still, he had to admit, it felt good when he took the pack off his back. But he knew he'd have plenty of time before summer to get used to hauling it around. He would start tomorrow. He'd wear the pack when he went out walking after school. Before long he'd hardly notice it. He could even add a tent—the little ones were only about five or six more pounds. By summertime he'd be ready to take the long hiking trip with the big guys at camp.

Of course, for next week, his framepack would just be like a medium-sized suitcase, just an easy way to carry stuff to his cabin at the state park.

Then Mark had a satisfying thought: When Mr. Maxwell saw him show up with all his gear, maybe the guy would know he wasn't looking at some little dork. Mr. Maxwell would see he was dealing with a kid who knew a thing or two about being outdoors.

There was another thought, a thought that Mark didn't even put into words. It was more like a hope that he kept hidden from himself. Because Mark hoped that when Mr. Maxwell saw him so pulled together, so serious, so well prepared, then the man would ease up, cut him some slack. He hoped the man would show him some respect.

Because Mark knew he deserved that.

Fourteen

Zero Tolerance

As the black Mercedes pulled into the school driveway at seven o'clock on Monday morning, Mark wished that he'd gotten up earlier, or maybe Leon should have driven faster. Because tons of other fifth-graders were already at the school.

Three big yellow buses sat at the curb, their doors open wide. Parked behind the buses there were five pickup trucks and four minivans. The cargo beds of the first two pickups were already loaded with luggage.

Mark saw a tall, rough-looking man talking with the principal. He had a clipboard, and so did Mrs. Gibson. She was pointing at the first bus, and the man was pointing at the second one.

With a start Mark realized what he was seeing. *That tall guy? That's Mr. Maxwell!*

He was wearing dark brown trousers, tan lace-up

hunting boots, a red flannel shirt, and a dark green jacket. His blaze orange cap was pulled down over a wild mess of graying brown hair, and it was plain to see that Mr. Maxwell had not shaved all weekend. He was headed for the woods.

A group of other cars pulled up behind them, and Leon said, "Out you go now. You have a good time, Mark. Or, how about *you* drive home, and *I* will go to the state park, eh?"

Mark grinned. "Sometime we'll go together, okay? And do some *real* camping. See you, Leon."

Leon popped the trunk open and Mark jumped out. He grabbed his pack and slung it onto his back. It was about three pounds heavier than it had been when he had tried it out in his room that first night. The extra weight wasn't because of the last few items from Mr. Survival's list—the space blanket, the extra flashlight batteries, and the other items weighed almost nothing. He'd found a couple of other neat things at Wal-Mart too, like the saw that was just a piece of rough wire with a ring on each end, and the plastic emergency poncho. But that stuff was real light too. The extra weight in his pack came from the school materials he was required to bring along.

By the time Mark got onto the sidewalk, about ten other kids were in line ahead of him, waiting to be checked in by Mr. Maxwell. Mark was surprised to see that two of the boys and one of the girls in the line had framepacks too.

He suddenly wished he'd just thrown his stuff into an old suitcase. Compared to the packs these kids had, his looked brand-new, because it was—and his was also a lot fancier. The fact that his pack was bright yellow didn't help. And the one-liter water bottles he had tucked into the mesh pockets on either side of his pack seemed silly now, unnecessary. Like he was showing off or something.

When it was his turn, Mr. Maxwell glanced at him, then ran a quick eye over his gear, and said, "Toss that into the fourth pickup and then get onto the first bus." That was it. No greeting, no comment, no smile.

On the bus Mark was glad to see Jason Frazier sitting near the back. He waved at Mark and then pointed at the seat across the aisle from him.

As Mark sat down Jason said, "Did you check out Old Man of the Mountain Maxwell?"

Mark nodded. "Yeah. I didn't even recognize him."

"Takes this whole deal pretty serious, y'know?" said Jason. "Sort of too much, maybe. But who cares? No school, man—that's what I like! And my brother said the food's good too. Not like the stuff at our cafeteria."

When the bus was almost full, Mrs. Stearns and Mrs. Leghorn got on. Mrs. Stearns smiled and joked with a group of girls sitting near the front of the bus. She had on hiking boots, jeans, and a hooded sweatshirt. She was in a good mood, and she was ready for the woods.

Mrs. Leghorn was wearing a pair of bright white tennis shoes, some pale purple slacks, and a long red wool coat with wide sleeves. A large black purse was looped over one arm, and in her other hand she kept a tight grip on a tall stainless steel coffee mug. She stood stiffly, flinching every time a kid yelled or laughed too loudly.

Mrs. Stearns called off the names from the list on her clipboard. Two kids hadn't arrived, but by the time she'd read off all the names, they had slipped aboard. The bus driver climbed on, buckled her seatbelt, yanked on the door lever, and as soon as Mrs. Stearns and Mrs. Leghorn took their seats, the bus lurched forward.

A Week in the Woods had officially begun.

When they arrived at Gray's Notch State Park, the boys on the first bus were divided up into three different groups. Mark and Jason and eight other boys were assigned to a one-room cabin called the Raven's Nest. A man named Mr. Frost—Jessica Frost's father—was their cabin chaperone. He looked nice enough to Mark, but he wasn't an outdoors type. More like a salesman, or maybe he worked in an office.

Mr. Frost helped the boys find all their luggage, and then he led the way down the campground road, past the restrooms and bath houses, past three RV slabs and two other cabins. Pointing at a log building

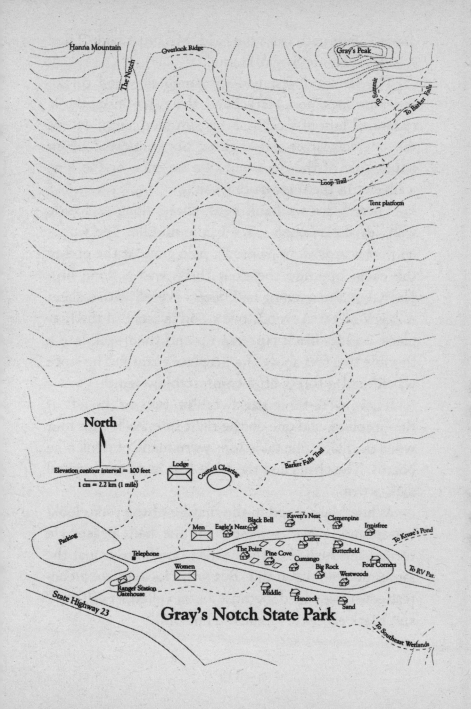

Hanna Mountain

The Notch

Overlook Ridge

Gray's Peak

To Summit

To Barker Falls

Loop Trail

Tent platform

Barker Falls Trail

North

Elevation contour interval = 100 feet

1 cm = 2.2 km (1 mile)

Lodge

Council Clearing

Black Bell

Raven's Nest

Clemenpine

Men

Eagle's Nest

Innisfree

Cutler

To Kruse's Pond

Parking

The Point

Pine Cove

Butterfield

Telephone

Cumango

Big Rock

Four Corners

To RV Par.

Women

Westwoods

Ranger Station
Gatehouse

Middle

Hancock

Sand

State Highway 23

Gray's Notch State Park

To Southeast Wetlands

down a short path from the road, Mr. Frost said, "Here it is guys, Home Sweet Home!"

The Raven's Nest had the smell of wood smoke and pine logs, and Mark liked the place instantly. It reminded him of a cabin at his summer camp, except this one was larger and brighter. Six windows, one on either side of the door and two on each of the long walls, let in the midmorning sun.

There were six bunk beds, three along each side wall, leaving an open space in the middle. The wooden floorboards were painted a pale gray. At the end of the cabin opposite the door there was a stone fireplace, but the opening had been covered with a sheet of black metal. A woodstove stood in front of the fireplace, and its black pipe ran up and then back into a thimble two feet above the fireplace mantel. The stove was lit and it threw off a comfortable warmth.

There were three sturdy tables, two on the left of the fireplace, and one on the right side, each with four wooden chairs. The table tops were made of thick pine boards. The chairs and the table legs had been painted dark green.

While Mark stood in the middle of the room looking around, a mad scramble for the beds began. He turned and rushed to the nearest bunk, arriving at the same moment Jason did. But what looked like a contest never happened, because Jason yelled, "I call top!" and Mark shouted, "I got the bottom!"

Amid the jumble and noise Mr. Frost said, "All right, boys, take it easy, now. Plenty of room for everyone. Get your sleeping bags unrolled, set out your shoes and boots, just sort of get settled in. And if you've got things to hang up like coats and jackets or towels, use the hooks on the walls, or the hooks on the ends of the bunks. Don't be throwing stuff around or dropping it wherever. We're going to be here a while, so keep things organized, okay? Now, on my schedule it says we've got some time here before the general meeting at the big lodge at eleven. But that doesn't mean you can wander off somewhere. No one goes anywhere unless I know about it first. And I mean *anywhere*. All week. We clear on that? Everyone?"

All the boys nodded, so Mr. Frost said, "Good. Now, most of your things should stay in your suitcases, and you should keep them pushed under your bunks so we're not tripping over them. So just get your stuff organized a little, and then we'll explore the area if there's time."

It turned out there wasn't time, because once everyone was settled in, Mr. Frost decided to organize a firewood brigade. "Listen up, guys. It's not going to get above fifty today, and it's going to be downright chilly tonight. So anybody who doesn't want to shiver all night, line up."

All ten boys from the Raven's Nest followed him down the road to the parking lot beside the gatehouse at the entrance to the campground. Mr. Maxwell had arranged to have two cords of split stove wood dumped there. The boys lined up beside the pile and Mr. Frost pulled back a corner of the big blue tarp and began to load wood onto the outstretched arms of the first couple of boys.

Jason was in front of Mark. Mr. Frost stacked three pieces of wood onto Jason's arms, and then he motioned to Mark. But Jason said, "I can carry more than this. Give me two more—at least!"

So Mr. Frost said, "Okay," and put on another two pieces of wood.

It was Mark's turn, and Mr. Frost put three pieces of wood on his arms and then said, "Next boy."

But Mark shook his head and said, "I can take at least two more pieces, maybe three."

Jason had turned to start walking back, but when he heard Mark say that, he looked over his shoulder and said, "Sure you can—in your dreams!"

But Mr. Frost shrugged and said, "Fine," and loaded Mark with two more chunks of wood.

When the last piece of wood was balanced on his stack, Mark turned and started walking. Jason was about twenty feet ahead of him. Mark lengthened his stride. After about thirty seconds he was only a step or two behind. Mark felt the muscles in his shoulders complain about the weight of the wood, felt his wrists ache from being bent upward at such an odd angle. But he didn't care. With a grim smile Mark notched his speed up a little higher.

As if he had radar, Jason glanced over his shoulder and saw Mark closing in. He grinned. "Oh no, you don't!" he said, and he sped up.

It was an all-out race. Every time Mark tried to pass him, Jason accelerated and swerved like a NASCAR driver. Both boys were huffing, their faces red from exertion, and they zoomed by the other two kids who had loaded up before them.

At the last second Mark surged forward and managed to get next to Jason. Shoulder to shoulder they reached the path that went left from the roadway back toward the Raven's Nest. The path went between two trees, and it was narrow, and Jason had the inside position. Mark had to give way—but he wouldn't, and he didn't.

The racers collided, their loads of wood clunking into the tree trunks and clattering to the ground as the boys tumbled into each other and collapsed into a gasping, laughing heap.

Jason reached over and gave Mark a friendly thump on the arm. "That was cheap! I had you all the way!"

"Yeah?" said Mark. "Then how come you're flat on your back?"

Jason didn't answer, and Mark sat up and turned to look at him. Jason was looking up over Mark's shoulder. He wasn't smiling.

Someone said, "You all right?"

Mark knew that voice. It was Mr. Maxwell.

The boys scrambled to their feet, and Jason said, "Oh sure, we're fine."

"We bumped into each other, that's all," said Mark, turning to face the man.

When Mr. Maxwell saw it was Mark, he scowled and then spoke gruffly. "Well, be more careful—both of you. Now get that mess cleared away." Then he turned on his heel and walked off toward the lodge.

Jason and Mark started picking up the wood.

When Mr. Maxwell was far enough away, Jason whispered, "I *still* beat you, loser!"

Mark whispered back, "Dream on—maybe you tied, but only because my wood was heavier than that little *baby* load of yours!"

Once their wood was stacked outside the door, Jason chased Mark into the cabin and they beat on each other with pillows until Mr. Frost arrived and added "No pillow fights" to his list of rules.

After the big meeting in the lodge, everyone ate lunch, had a restroom break, and then gathered outside in the council clearing at one o'clock. All the kids sat on logs that were arranged in a series of expanding circles. It was like an outdoor auditorium, and the stage was in the center. Except it wasn't a stage, just an open space with a stone fire pit. Next to the fire pit there was a big iron bell mounted on a sturdy wooden post.

Once everyone was settled Mr. Maxwell said, "We're going to start off our Week in the Woods with the annual Nature Study Scavenger Hunt. Here's how it works."

Then he explained that they would split into teams made up of one boys cabin and one girls cabin—about twenty kids and three or four grown-ups each. Every team would get the same list of seventy-five things to search for—little things like an acorn, a piece of mica, a white oak leaf, a pine cone, a piece of quartz, a piece of granite, a shred of birch bark, an aspen leaf, a maple twig—on and on. Mr. Maxwell explained the special rules designed to keep the park from being trampled or ripped up, especially rules about where to search and how to collect the samples. For example, all the plant samples had to be picked up off the ground, never from living trees or bushes. Each team had to stay in a certain area of the campground. Plus, every hunter had to keep a written record of where each object had been picked up so that everything could be returned to its right place in the ecosystem after the hunt.

After all the explanations Mr. Maxwell said, "There's a one-hour time limit, and you've all got a lot of things to find. So let's get going!" Then he pretended to remember something. "Oh! I almost forgot to tell you: Members of the *last*-place team will have to help serve and clear the tables at dinner tonight. And everybody on the *winning* team is going to get an extra helping of dessert! So is everyone ready?"

A hundred and fifty kids yelled, "Yeah!" Mr. Maxwell rang the bell, and the hunt was on.

For an hour the woods around the campground echoed with the shouts and yells of the hunters.

"Quartz! I've got a chunk of quartz!"

"Hey, quick! Over here! I found a birch branch on the ground!"

Squads of kids picked their way carefully through the search areas. There were arguments and discussions, notes were scribbled into the logbooks, and as time ran out, the pace intensified. And all the while, the parents and teachers kept careful watch to be sure no one strayed off into the woods in search of that perfect granite pebble or a missing hemlock cone.

When the big bell at the council clearing rang at two fifteen, all the teams gathered for the judging. That part of the event was almost as noisy as the collecting had been. It went quickly, with three teams of judges moving from group to group. There was a lot of cheering and clapping, and there were more arguments, too. Disputes about what would count and what wouldn't were settled by Mr. Maxwell.

Mark watched carefully as the judges went over his team's collection. He and Jason had worked as a pair, and together they had found eighteen items for the team. All together, their group had found sixty-two of the seventy-five things on the list before time ran out.

But they didn't win. Another team had found sixty-seven. They wouldn't be having an extra dessert, but they wouldn't have to clear the tables, either.

At three o'clock Mark and his cabin mates headed back to the Raven's Nest for a half-hour break before the next activity. The cabin had cooled off a little, so Mr. Frost got the poker off the wall by the fireplace, opened the door of the stove, and raked some live coals toward the front of the firebox. Then he put a couple of small logs into the stove, shut the door, and began to fiddle with the airflow adjustment.

Mark sat down on his bed. After unlacing his hiking boots, he pulled his pack out from under the bunk to look for his Jack London book. Jason sat down at the other end of Mark's mattress and started rooting around in his suitcase.

Just as Mark found his book, Jason whispered, "Hey, Mark, check this out." Looking around carefully, he reached toward Mark with something in his hand. Mark put out his hand, and as he took it, Jason whispered, "Turn toward me so no one sees it."

Mark held the thing close to his body and took a quick look down. It was a brown leather case, about four inches long, an inch and a half wide, and one inch thick. The flap on the front was held shut with a round copper snap. There had once been some gold lettering on the flap, but it was mostly worn away. The thing weighed a lot, almost half a pound.

"Go on," urged Jason, "take it out."

Mark tugged the snap open, lifted the flap, and pulled out something made of stainless steel. Turning it over in his hands, it looked like two separate rectangles of metal, hinged together at one end. Then Mark knew what it was. He'd seen things like this on the REI Web site. They called them "multitools."

He nodded at Jason and whispered, "Cool!" Taking hold at the end opposite the hinge, Mark pulled the sides of the tool outward, folded them all the way around, and in two seconds the object was transformed into a pair of sturdy needle-nose pliers. "This is great!" And it was. The tool was wonderfully made, solid and heavy in his hand.

The door of the cabin slammed, and Mark turned instinctively toward the sound. Then he quickly turned back and tucked the tool under his leg.

Mr. Maxwell stood in the doorway. He talked to the whole cabin, but his eyes kept coming back to Mark. "How's it going here in the Raven's Nest? Looks like you've got everything you need. I'm just checking every cabin to make sure everyone's comfortable. You guys are great, though. Got a fire going, got your woodpile started—looks like you're all set!"

Mr. Frost was on his feet, smiling at Mr. Maxwell. "We're doing fine, just fine. Terrific bunch of boys here. And we can't wait for dinner!"

"Won't be long now," said Mr. Maxwell, "right

after your meetings with the subject teachers. I'll see you all there, okay?"

He turned, put his hand on the doorknob, and then hesitated.

Turning back around, he walked over to Mark. He pointed down at the bunk and said, "Unless I'm mistaken, you're hiding something under your leg there. Am I mistaken?"

Mark gulped. Then he shook his head. "No. You're right. It's a tool." And he reached under his leg, picked it up, and held it out.

Mr. Maxwell took it from him. In his big hands the tool looked like a toy. He turned it over once or twice. Then he bent the ends around and folded the pliers back into the handles.

Holding it up between his big thumb and forefinger, Mr. Maxwell wagged the tool at Mark and said, "I'm sorry I found this. You shouldn't have this here." Nodding at the bed he said, "Hand me the sheath."

Mark gave it to him.

Pointing below the bunk Mr. Maxwell said, "Grab your pack and get all your stuff into it."

Mark was confused. "All my stuff? Why?"

"Why?" said Mr. Maxwell. "I'll tell you why. Because of this." And holding the tool in one hand he flipped at the edge with his thumb. Out popped a four-inch blade. "*This* is a knife. And the instructions for A Week in the Woods said no student was to bring a knife of any kind. But it's more than that. Because this is a school-sponsored event. So this is really school, just like a field trip or an assembly. And our district has a zero-tolerance rule about bringing weapons to school. So this, this *knife* means you are going to be suspended from school."

Mr. Maxwell folded the knife blade back into the handle, put the tool into its case, and then dropped it into his jacket pocket. "So like I said, pack up all your stuff. Now. You know what my truck looks like? The old blue GMC?"

Almost in a daze, Mark nodded.

Mr. Maxwell said, "It's parked in the lot by the gatehouse. Toss your stuff in the back and wait for me in the cab. You're going home."

Then Mr. Maxwell turned and walked out the door.

Except for the metallic creaking of the woodstove, it was silent in the Raven's Nest. Mark's face was burning hot. Feeling as if he was moving in a dream, he stood up, turned around, bent down, and started rolling his sleeping bag.

Jason jumped to his feet. Mark looked up, and Jason pointed at himself, mouthing the words, "I should tell."

Mark shook his head. "No," he whispered. "I'm the one who got caught. I'll get in less trouble than you would. Really. It's okay."

It took Mark less than three minutes to load his

pack and strap the rolled sleeping bag to the bottom. He stepped clear of the bunk, swung the pack around onto his back, and walked to the door. Stopping, he looked back, glancing from face to face around the room. He saw a lot of pale faces, even a couple of watery eyes.

Forcing a thin smile to his lips, Mark said, "See you, guys . . . sorry."

Then he left.

Fifteen

Retrial

It took Mr. Maxwell about fifteen minutes to locate Mrs. Stearns. After checking over at the girl's cabins, he walked back and found her at the main lodge.

Taking her aside, he explained what he had to do. "And I'm going to have to leave you in charge for a couple of hours, all right?"

"My *goodness*," she said, shaking her head. "You'd think that boy would have more sense than to do something so stupid. But sooner or later everybody's got to learn that 'no' means 'no,' even when your daddy's got half a billion dollars. I'll keep things on track here, Bill, but please hurry back."

Walking along the roadway toward the gatehouse, Mr. Maxwell assured himself that he was doing the right thing. *The rules are the rules, and they've got to be obeyed*, he said to himself. *I can't make an exception here, not even if I wanted to.*

And the odd thing was, part of Mr. Maxwell wanted to. He almost wished he could let Mark off the hook.

He had watched Mark earlier during the scavenger hunt. The boy really got into it. Such a difference from the way he'd been acting in science class! Of course, lately Mr. Maxwell knew that he hadn't been any help at all, hadn't exactly been encouraging Mark to participate. He'd been stiff-arming the kid every chance he got.

But watching Mark this afternoon, seeing him scramble around through the brush, laughing and shouting to his friends, Mr. Maxwell's heart had begun to soften a little. He'd been tempted to consider giving the kid another chance—not wipe the slate clean or anything, but just ease up on him a bit and see what would happen.

And now this.

Mr. Maxwell kept quizzing himself, testing his motives. He asked himself, *If it had been some other kid, would I have reacted like this? Or would I have just said, "Nice tool, but you better let me keep it till the week is over." Would I?*

But the fact was, it wasn't some other kid. It was *this* kid, Mark Robert Chelmsley. *And if I did let him off on this, it wouldn't be good for him.* That's what Mr. Maxwell told himself, and he believed it. It was like Mrs. Stearns had said: Everybody's got to learn about obeying rules, and sometimes you have to learn the hard way.

At the door of the gatehouse, Mr. Maxwell paused, his hand on the knob. Looking across the wide parking lot he could see the roof of his blue pickup, and he thought of the boy sitting in the front seat. And he thought, *Kid's been over there stewing in his own juices for twenty minutes now. Maybe that's been enough. Maybe he's learned his lesson.* But his years of experience kicked in and said, *No. Discipline isn't discipline unless you follow through and make it stick.*

Inside, the ranger was on the phone. "Yeah . . . I'll hold." Covering the mouthpiece, he said, "Hey, Bill! Good to see ya!"

Mr. Maxwell nodded and smiled as he leaned across the counter and shook the man's hand.

Pointing at the phone, the ranger said, "Only be a minute here." Speaking into the phone again, he said, "Hey, Tommy! It's Jim Pletcher, over at Gray's Notch. . . . Yeah, pretty good. Tell me, d'you think you could get a vacuum truck over here tomorrow morning? I think the pit behind the main sanitary unit must have picked up some groundwater over the winter. . . .Yeah, been some complaints. . . . Yup, that's what it smells like. . . . 'preciate it, Tommy. See you tomorrow."

Hanging up, he turned to Mr. Maxwell, smiling broadly. "Sorry I missed you this morning. Looks like a great gang of kids. Just like old times, every spring. Now, what can I do ya for?"

"Just need to use the phone, Jim. Got sort of an emergency."

"Jeeze, Bill! Shoulda told me to hang up!" Handing Mr. Maxwell the receiver, he said, "Here—anything I can help with? You need a vehicle or anything?"

"No, no, it's not a real emergency, Jim. Just a kid who's going home. Kind of a smart-mouth rich kid—thinks the rules are for everyone else. Little bit of a tough guy."

"What, he start a fight or somethin'?" asked the ranger. "Take a poke at you?"

"No, nothing like that," said Mr. Maxwell. "He had a knife."

"Jeeze! Kid come at you with a knife?! Did he cut ya?"

Mr. Maxwell shook his head and put his hands up. "Whoa, Jim, slow down. He didn't come at me with anything. He just had the knife with him. It's a Leatherman, one of the big ones." Mr. Maxwell took the tool out of his pocket and laid it on the counter.

The ranger picked it up and took it out of its sheath. Turning it over a few times in his hands, he squinted at it. Glancing up at the teacher, he said, "Jeeze, Bill. It isn't really *that* big, is it? And it's more of a tool, too. The kid's gettin' sent home for this? Gonna miss the whole week?"

Mr. Maxwell nodded. "It's a weapons rule. Probably be suspended, too. No knives at any school activity."

The ranger studied the tool again and then squinted up into Mr. Maxwell's face. "Even here at a state park? In the woods and all? I'm not telling you how to run your program here, Bill, but that seems pretty rough. Did you give the kid a chance to say he was sorry or anything? I mean, I could talk to him, if you want me to—y'know, be extra serious and everything? When I get my hat on I can look real official, throw a good scare into him if you want. What d'you say? I'm sure I can get through to him. What's the boy's name?"

Mr. Maxwell smiled and shook his head. "His name is Mark, and I thank you, Jim, but I know this kid. Somebody's got to come down hard on him. Might as well be me. Best thing for him. Um . . . would you mind stepping outside for a minute? This won't take long. It'll be a toll call, but the school'll pay for it."

The ranger nodded and went out the door, still holding on to the tool.

When the ranger came back inside a minute later, Mr. Maxwell was talking on the phone, trying not to lose his temper. "Yes, I understand that Mr. Chelmsley isn't home right now, but surely you've got a number where he could be reached. . . . I know it's later over there, but I'm sure he'd want me to wake him up. This is important."

The ranger motioned for Mr. Maxwell to cover the mouthpiece. Then he said, "Bill, tell those folks you'll call 'em right back, okay?"

Mr. Maxwell shook his head. "Jim, I'm handling this. I appreciate what you're trying to do, but—"

The ranger put his hand on Mr. Maxwell's arm and looked him in the eye. "Bill, just tell 'em you'll call back. Go on, tell 'em that. Right now."

Lips pressed tightly together, Mr. Maxwell took his hand off the mouthpiece and said, "Hello? Yes, I'm sorry. I'm going to have to call you back, all right? . . . Yes, everything's fine. . . . Yes, Mark is fine. I'll call you back. Good-bye."

Turning to squarely face the ranger, Mr. Maxwell said, "Jim, I know you—"

"Bill," said the ranger, holding up his hand, "forget all that, and just answer me one question: This boy's name is Mark—what's his last name?"

"Chelmsley," snapped Mr. Maxwell. "His last name is Chelmsley, but I've already told you . . ."

The ranger held up his hand again. "Hear me out, Bill. If this boy's name is Mark Chelmsley, then what do you make of this?"

Handing the knife to Mr. Maxwell, the ranger pointed at the flat side of the handle. Mr. Maxwell had to hold the knife almost at arm's length, and when he did and tilted it to catch the light, he saw what the ranger was talking about. Something was scratched into the brushed finish on the stainless steel, some crude letters. Squinting, he looked again, and the letters snapped into focus: Jason Frazier.

"Jason Frazier!" Mr. Maxwell let out a long breath and sank into the chair at the desk. "This is *terrible*!"

The ranger watched Mr. Maxwell, watched the waves of thought roll across his face. First amazement, then relief. Then something that the ranger had to call pain—deep pain.

"This is awful, Jim! I've been mad at this kid for weeks because he's kind of spoiled and he's got a smart mouth, and today I jump all over him about this knife and I'm about to send him home and get him suspended from school. And all he's doing is taking the heat for his friend—that's Jason. In his cabin. This is awful! I've got to go talk to him."

The ranger nodded understandingly, both men feeling a little embarrassed at the sudden burst of emotion. "Sure. Absolutely, Bill. Go talk to him. Or, if you want, I'll go to his cabin and bring 'im so you can talk here. Be more private, if you want."

Mr. Maxwell nodded toward the parking lot. "Thanks, but he's right over there in my truck. Been sitting there sweating bullets for half an hour now."

The ranger said, "Well, go on, then. You've got good news for him, right?"

"I sure do. Good news." Mr. Maxwell stood up and reached out a hand, and the ranger took it in a strong handshake. Looking the man in the face, Mr. Maxwell said, "I owe you for this, Jim. I owe you a lot."

"Nah, forget it, Bill."

Walking across the parking lot, Bill Maxwell knew what he was going to do. First he was going to apologize. He was going to tell Mark he was proud of him. He was going to tell Mark that loyalty is just about the finest quality a person can have. He was going to tell Mark how badly he had misjudged him—about a lot of things, probably. And he was going to ask the boy to forgive him.

Mr. Maxwell rounded the back of his truck, a big smile on his face, and he took three quick strides and grabbed the handle of the passenger-side door.

But then he froze. He didn't open the door. And he stopped smiling.

Mark wasn't in the truck.

Sixteen

Into the Woods

Walking back past the gatehouse, Mr. Maxwell forced himself to give the ranger a smile and a thumbs-up. But that wasn't how he felt. Mark wasn't in the truck.

So the first thing Mr. Maxwell had to do was go to Mark's cabin and see if maybe he'd swung back there. Maybe Mark had forgotten something. Or maybe he'd be at the washrooms. That made sense.

Fifteen minutes later Mr. Maxwell had looked everywhere he could think of—the Raven's Nest, the other cabins, the washrooms, the lodge, the kitchen, the campground roadways, everywhere.

Back at the gatehouse Mr. Maxwell told the ranger that he hadn't found the boy. Then he asked, "Would you have seen him if he went to my truck out there in the lot? I mean, could he have walked past here without you noticing, do you think?"

The ranger heard the fear in Mr. Maxwell's voice.

He didn't answer right away. Narrowing his eyes, he said, "Bill, are you thinkin' that this boy's run off? 'Cause if he has, then we've got a real problem. I haven't been sleepin' any this afternoon, but if you're askin' me could a kid have slipped by here and got down the entrance road and out onto the state highway, then sure, he could've done that. So I'm telling you that we need to jump on this, like right now. 'Cause we've got some bad possibilities, and then we've got some terrible ones. Like if he went out to the highway and somebody picked him up."

Mr. Maxwell felt the sweat break out on his forehead. "Listen, Jim. Give me twenty minutes, okay? I just want to make a quick pass back through the campground, and if I don't get any news, then I'll turn it all over to you, okay?"

The ranger rubbed his chin a second or two and then said, "Fifteen minutes. You get back to me in fifteen minutes with good news or I've got to start makin' phone calls."

"Fair enough, Jim. Thanks." And Mr. Maxwell was out the door at a trot.

On his first quick search, Mr. Maxwell had been past all the girls' cabins, but he hadn't talked to all the chaperones and teachers, hadn't actually asked if anyone had set eyes on Mark Chelmsley carrying a bright yellow backpack, headed toward the parking lots. Now he was asking.

The grown-ups in the first three cabins hadn't seen

a thing. Then in the Pine Cove cabin he talked with Mrs. Leghorn. She was sitting in a chair close to the woodstove, her long red coat tucked around her legs, her stainless steel coffee cup in her gloved hands.

"Mark?" she said. "Yes, I saw him. I was walking to the kitchen for some coffee, and he went across the path. Had that big thing on his back."

Mr. Maxwell's heart took a leap, but he kept his voice calm and low. "Were you at the lodge when you saw him?"

Mrs. Leghorn shook her head. "Not quite. I was almost to the council clearing, in the woods on this side of it." Motioning with her hands, she said, "I was walking this way, toward the lodge, and he cut across ahead of me at the near end of the clearing, kind of going that way."

Mr. Maxwell leaned forward. "You're sure about that? He wasn't walking toward the road?"

Mrs. Leghorn shook her head. "No, I'm sure. He wasn't headed toward the road at all."

Mr. Maxwell knew Gray's Notch State Park almost as well as he knew his own forty-five acres. And he knew that if Mrs. Leghorn and Mark had crossed paths where she said they had, and if Mark hadn't been heading for the road, there was only one other place he could have been going.

Mr. Maxwell said, "Listen, Elsa, I need you to do something for me, right now, okay? I need you to walk to the gatehouse as quickly as you can and tell the ranger that I've found Mark, all right?"

Taking a last sip of coffee, Mrs. Leghorn stood up and said, "Of course, Bill. Was he lost or something?"

Mr. Maxwell nodded. "Sort of. Tell Jim—that's the ranger—tell him that Mark walked up the Barker Falls Trail, and that I've gone to fetch him, and that we'll be back soon, all right? Got that?"

The math teacher nodded. "Barker Falls Trail."

Mr. Maxwell said, "Right," and with that he turned, rushed out the door, veered to the left, and began jogging toward the trailhead at the east edge of the council clearing.

Mark eased himself down until he was sitting on a boulder, his breath coming in rough gasps. For more than an hour he'd been pushing himself pretty hard. He unhooked the straps, shrugged off his pack, then bent down to get a water bottle. Unscrewing the cap, he took a long drink. Right away he wished he hadn't. *I should probably be more careful with my water.* He dug into his pack and pulled out an energy bar. He opened the end of the wrapper, took one bite, then carefully tucked it away again.

Mark was in good shape, so it didn't take him long to catch his breath. After about two minutes he stood up and stretched. His right heel felt a little warm, but he didn't think it was starting to blister. Besides, there was no time for first aid, not now. He picked up his pack, settled the pads on his shoulders, fastened the strap across his chest, and then snapped the buckle of the waist belt.

He looked back at the rocky ravine he had just climbed, and then ahead into the pines and the leafless groves of maple and birch that covered the rising ground on both sides of the trail. Suddenly Mark felt small.

It wasn't like feeling small compared to another kid. It wasn't like feeling small in the crowd during a Knicks game at Madison Square Garden. This was different, a new kind of small.

High overhead a crow called, and Mark tipped his face up to scan the gray sky above the treetops. A second crow answered the first, and he saw them both, winging north. *Or is that east?* he asked himself.

Mark wasn't sure. He almost reached for his compass, because then he could figure it out. Wouldn't be hard to do. Then he could at least be sure of something.

Because Mark wasn't sure of much at that moment. He wasn't sure if anyone would find him. He wasn't sure if anyone was looking yet. He wasn't sure how far he had walked since the last trail marker.

But glancing at his watch, he was suddenly sure of one thing: It was two minutes after four, and if anyone *was* coming after him, he didn't have time to be standing around.

Mark turned and started walking uphill again.

* * *

"I'll get in less trouble than you would."

That's what Mark had whispered to Jason in the Raven's Nest. And at that moment, Mark felt sure it was true.

This whole thing is stupid anyway. It's not like I was waving the knife around or trying to kill someone with it. I didn't even know the thing had a blade! And if Mr. Maxwell had found Jason with it, would Jason be getting sent home? No way. This is about me and Mr. Maxwell. Mark had felt sure of that, too.

And how much trouble am I really in? After all, this isn't even my school, not really. Or my town. Suspended for a week? Or even for the rest of the year? So what? That's what Mark had told himself in the cabin as he rolled his sleeping bag and gathered his things.

But when he had gotten outside, when he had started walking toward the parking lot, Mark didn't feel so confident. Walking on the path, dragging his boots on the ground, scraping up a small heap of pine needles with every step, Mark felt the weight of the situation pressing in from all sides. *What are Mom and Dad going to say about this?* he asked himself. *And what if Mr. Maxwell or the principal calls Runyon Academy? What then?*

And then there was the fact that he was going to miss the whole Week in the Woods. Walking on the roadway now, a deep wave of self-pity surged up in

141

Mark's chest, and he had to gulp hard to keep from letting out a sob. *It's not fair!* he raged, and the feeling was so intense that for a moment Mark thought he had screamed the words out loud.

Then a thought stopped him in his tracks. *I've got to go and wait in Mr. Maxwell's truck? That's because he's going to drive me home himself! He wants to! He wants to rub it in and watch me squirm, all the way home!*

Turning to his right, Mark looked around. There was no one in sight. Then at the edge of the council clearing Mark saw the big brown display board he had looked at earlier during the scavenger hunt. It was the starting point of a ten-mile trail that went up to a waterfall.

Mark walked toward the trailhead, his stride getting longer and more purposeful with every step. He didn't hesitate, didn't falter, didn't slow his pace. And as he passed the display board and saw the first red trail marker nailed to a tree twenty yards ahead, he said to himself, *If Mr. Maxwell wants to get rid of me so bad, then he's gonna have to find me first!*

Seventeen

Tracks

Mr. Maxwell stopped jogging once he got to the trail. He didn't want to work up a sweat, didn't want his shirt to feel wet. It wasn't that cold yet, only about fifty, but he knew the temperature would drop as the trail went up Gray's Mountain toward Barker Falls. Plus the sun would be going down. And damp clothes in cold weather means trouble for a hiker.

Mr. Maxwell settled into a steady pace, counting on his longer stride to quickly eat up the distance between himself and Mark Chelmsley. He did the mental calculations. *Soft suburban kid, carrying a pack, walking uphill—can't be making more than three miles an hour.* At every bend in the trail Mr. Maxwell expected to see Mark sitting on a log, worn out and footsore, waiting to be rescued.

He had no doubts about being on the right trail.

Even if the boy hadn't been one of the first hikers on the trail this season, and even if his child-sized boots hadn't left distinctive ridged prints on the softer pieces of ground, Mr. Maxwell would still have been able to follow Mark's trail as easily as a trucker follows the highway. Tracking was one of his specialties.

Mr. Maxwell was proud of his woodcraft. He felt he understood nature. He knew the outdoors from both sides.

On the theoretical side, he had studied nature as a scientist. He had learned about the plants and creatures of the great northern forest. He had learned about the processes that shaped the landscape. He had learned about the systems of the natural world and how they worked together.

On the practical side, he understood the day-to-day rhythms of nature. He had that quiet understanding of the woods and mountains that comes only after years of experience on the ground.

Some of Bill Maxwell's friends didn't understand how he could be so concerned about conservation and still be a hunter. That's because they didn't get up with him at four in the morning on a crisp fall day and leave the house with nothing but a hunting bow and one razor-tipped arrow. They didn't hike with him for two hours in the predawn silence, watching for deer spoor, finding the right place to wait, sometimes for five or six hours, a place where he could blend with the woods, notice every motion, every change in wind direction, every small sound, waiting for a buck to step into his line of sight.

They didn't understand that moment of silently fitting the arrow to the string, slowly drawing it back past his right ear, muscles tensed, aiming at that spot just above the front shoulder of the deer. It wasn't a moment of selfishness. It was a moment of admitting his connection with all of nature, of admitting his dependence on it. It was a moment of gratitude, of reverence for life.

And those people who disapproved of hunting didn't understand that for years now, after taking aim, Bill Maxwell would slowly ease the bowstring back to a straight line, make a small noise, and smile as the startled deer bolted into the brush. He didn't take the food nature offered him because he didn't truly need it. He only needed to know that the food was still there.

Mr. Maxwell usually did his best thinking as he walked alone in the woods. It usually calmed him down and helped him clear his mind. Not today. Today his thoughts were a tangle of fear and worry. And most of all, guilt.

Pigheaded idiot, that's what I am, he said to himself. *Got all bent out of shape because some eleven-year-old kid wouldn't jump through hoops for me. Had to be the big tough guy and get back at him. Way to go!*

And the farther Mr. Maxwell walked along the trail, looking down now and then at the small boot prints of the boy, the worse he felt.

Mark was alone with his thoughts too.

For a long time he had held on to his anger. He focused only on keeping up his pace. But after more than an hour and a half, Mark realized that someone *must* be looking for him by now. But of course, no one would know where to start.

Mark imagined the commotion. People running around, searching all the cabins, calling his name. And Mr. Maxwell would probably be in tons of trouble for letting a kid get lost. *Lost! That's a good one*, thought Mark with a smile.

But then he thought, *Maybe they've called the police. And Leon and Anya. And my parents. Because they think I'm lost. And maybe the school will have to cancel the whole program, send all the kids home tomorrow so they can search. For me.*

And that brought Mark to a complete stop at a bend in the trail. The seriousness of what he was doing struck him full force. He was mad at Mr. Maxwell, but he didn't want to ruin the week for everyone else. Plus get himself in more and more trouble.

Mark sat on the trunk of a big fallen pine tree that lay along one side of the trail. He shrugged off his pack and unzipped the outer pouch. He rustled through his school papers until he found what he wanted: the map Mrs. Farr had handed out in social studies. It was a map of the whole park. It wasn't printed very clearly, but Mark found the Barker Falls Trail. He identified the spur that he'd seen a while back that headed off to the right. It went about a quarter of a mile to a tent platform.

And sitting there studying the map, Mark saw a way back. But it wasn't just a way back. It was a way *out*, out of the mess he'd started to stir up. The map showed a trail that looped off to the left from the main trail and wound back down to the campground. This loop trail ended up on the far side of the main lodge, away from all the cabins and the council clearing, almost to the parking lots. *Perfect!* he thought. *I take that trail back down, spend the night close to the campground, and then show up in the morning! All I have to do is wander out of the woods over by the parking lot— maybe act like I got lost!*

And then Mark thought that maybe he should let himself be found tonight. *No sense making everyone worry all night. All I have to do is find that trail. It's right here on the map. It has to be close by.*

Happy with this decision, Mark allowed himself another drink of water and the rest of the energy bar he had nibbled on earlier.

As he stood up and turned around to pull on his pack, Mark saw the trail. It was right there, just behind where he'd been sitting. The big pine tree had almost hidden it, but now Mark saw it clear as day, angling off to the left. He stepped up onto the log, jumped down on the far side, and set off along the trail, his heart much lighter and his mind at peace.

At five o'clock Mr. Maxwell stopped to catch his breath and evaluate the situation. As he ran down the facts, he counted them off on his fingers.

Fact: I've come about three and a half miles from camp.

Fact: No boy in sight.

Fact: The trail's getting harder—steeper and rockier.

Fact: Mark has to be close now, he has to be worn out.

Fact: It's cloudy, but it won't start to get dark until seven or so.

Fact: If I find Mark in the next hour, we can get back to camp before dark.

The last two facts got Mr. Maxwell moving again. Time was running out. It was going to get cold tonight, probably down below freezing. In an hour he'd have to turn back whether he'd found Mark or not. That would mean the boy would have to spend the night alone on the mountain. And Mr. Maxwell found that thought unacceptable. He fastened the top button of his jacket and set off again, picking up his pace.

Ten minutes later Mr. Maxwell lost Mark's tracks. No boot prints. Doubling back about two hundred yards, he found the problem. A big pine tree had been cut down and the log had been laid along the left side of the main trail. And there were Mark's prints. Mr. Maxwell could see that Mark had sat down and taken off his pack. Then he'd stood up, stepped up onto the log, and gone off onto the other side. He'd taken the side trail.

Mr. Maxwell looked at the tracks, and then looked at the trail heading off to the left. And he took a deep breath and let it out slowly.

Mr. Maxwell knew that trail. He'd hiked it lots of times. It was a loop trail. It looped around back to the campground, but not directly. That trail went across the side of the mountain and then up steeply to a high ridge before it cut back down. The views were beautiful, so beautiful that the trail had been overused—too many hikers. And then the heavy spring rains had caused some serious erosion. Some dangerous erosion.

The thick pine log had been laid across the head of the trail for a reason. That trail had been closed for three years.

Eighteen

Bushwhacking

Mark was glad Anya had made him take his stocking cap.

He'd been hiking on the loop trail for about half an hour. A stiff breeze had come up, making the brisk air feel much colder. He'd had to stop and fish the hat out of the zippered compartment on the top of his pack, and now his ears were warm again.

The scrub oak trees on either side of the trail still held some of their dry leaves from the previous fall, and when the gusts swept up the hillside, the rustling sound reminded Mark of waves breaking along a beach. The bare branches of the maple and birch trees swayed and tapped against each other, and high overhead where the wind was stronger, the pine trees waved and sighed.

Mark noticed from the start that this loop trail

wasn't nearly as wide as the main trail had been. He had to keep a sharp lookout for the markers. The ones on this trail were blue, and there weren't as many of them. Sometimes they were almost hidden by tree branches. A few times when the trail wasn't obvious, Mark searched until he found the next little blue circle, or the next splotch of faded blue paint on a rock. And it didn't help that in some places the pine and hemlock trees were thick enough to dim the fading daylight.

Mark tried not to think about it, but his pack had begun to feel heavier. A lot heavier. Mark knew he was getting tired. He knew he was slowing down some, too. *But that's okay*, he thought. *I'm just going back to the campground, and even if it gets dark, I've got a flashlight. And the trail is mostly downhill, right?* So Mark ignored his body's call for rest. He kept pushing ahead.

As Mark walked out of a thick grove of birch and hemlock trees, the trail made a sharp turn to his right, angling up across a stretch of mostly open hillside. Only a few scruffy oaks and low junipers clung to the slope. The climb would be steep, but that wasn't the problem. The problem was that the trail wasn't really a trail anymore. It looked more like the rocky bed of an uphill river. Where the trail used to be there was a crazy jumble of granite boulders, some of them as big as washing machines. To go up that way, Mark saw he'd have to pick out a path either above the gullied trail, or just below it.

Or, he thought, *I could find a different way.*

Mark dug the map out of his pants pocket and unfolded it. He saw the sharp turn that the trail took on the map and thought, *So that means I'm right here.* The trail headed uphill for a stretch, then went left for a half mile along a ridge, and then the trail turned left once more and went almost straight downhill toward the campground.

Mark looked uphill at the boulders. And then turning left to face the hemlock and birch grove, he thought, *According to the map, if I just go straight that way, then in about half a mile I'll come to the trail again, the part that heads down to the campground. Then I won't have to fight my way uphill at all.* It seemed simple to Mark, especially since he was tired and hungry and his legs and feet and shoulders were hurting. Then he thought, *Still, I'd better use my compass.*

So he took off his pack once more, pulled his compass out of the front pouch, and did some quick thinking. The map showed that the uphill part of the trail was heading north. Then at the ridge, the trail made a left turn, which meant it would be heading roughly west; and since the trail turned left again to go downhill, that would mean it was running almost straight south. *So from where I'm standing,* Mark said to himself, *I go west, and that'll take me directly across to the downhill part of the trail. I get to the trail, and turn left, which is south. Simple.*

With a groan Mark heaved his pack up onto his back and fastened the buckles and straps. He looped the lanyard of his compass over his head. Then he opened the cover of the compass and turned the whole thing until the red end of the magnetic needle lined up with the N on the case. Then keeping the compass still and steady, Mark turned himself until north was to his right, and he was facing toward the letter W on the compass case—due west.

And then Mark started walking. Working his way westward, Mark found that the going was a lot harder. It wasn't like walking on a trail. He had to duck under low branches, step over fallen limbs and trees, and push his way through tangled brush. His framepack felt even heavier, and it kept getting caught on things as he worked his way forward. There were occasional rocky stretches where there was less brush, but picking his way among the rocks and outcroppings wasn't easy either.

Mark had checked his compass every thirty steps or so. He had also taken care not to drift downhill to his left as he walked across the shoulder of the mountain. When large outcroppings or dense brush had pushed him off course, he had always adjusted for the detour and gotten himself going due west again—

straight toward the trail that would lead him back to camp. And Mark had tried his best to count his steps and estimate his distance. He had done everything right.

That's why, after thirty minutes of walking, Mark couldn't understand why he hadn't found the trail yet. After forty-five minutes he began to wonder if his compass was working properly. And after almost an hour Mark thought maybe Mrs. Farr's map was wrong. So he stopped to look at it again.

But it wasn't the map's fault. And Mark's compass wasn't to blame. It was the forest. The forest had tricked him—that, plus his own inexperience.

A more experienced hiker would have known that a log laid across a trailhead means "trail closed." If Mark had known that, then maybe he wouldn't have been looking for a trail that was wide and clear and worn away like the other one had been. And if Mark had known that the trail he was trying to find had been closed for three years, then he might have kept a more careful lookout for it. Because three years is a long time in the forest.

For the past three years every tree and plant along-side the unused trail had stretched its branches out into the open space, reaching for more light—first the ferns and the scrub oak and the blueberry bushes, then the evergreens and the hardwoods. And on the trail bed itself the winged maple seeds and the pine cones and the acorns and the layers of roots had been hard at work, trying to reclaim their ground. The seedlings and the runners had sent their roots into the boot-softened soil to soak up the water that pooled on the path after every rain. Without the almost daily pounding of hiking boots, new plants and shoots had grown and flourished.

And that's why, at the particular place where Mark had crossed the downhill leg of the loop trail, his eyes saw only more forest.

After looking at Mrs. Farr's map and then looking at his watch again, Mark realized that somehow, somewhere he must have missed the trail. So he made a good decision. He decided to backtrack. He turned himself around, checked his compass, and headed due east.

As he walked, Mark thought back to Saturday, just two nights ago. He'd gone outside after dinner to mess around down by the little pond behind his house, and he'd watched the sunset at about seven fifteen. It had stayed light for quite a while after that. That's because on Saturday the sky had been clear. Not today. Today the clouds were thick and dark. It was only quarter of seven, and the daylight was fading fast. And it was also getting colder.

Instinctively Mark picked up his pace. He wanted to find the trail down to the campground before dark. Mark took forty steps, and stopped to check his compass. Another forty steps, another compass check.

It was when Mark stopped to check his compass the fifth time.

From far ahead and uphill, sort of off to his left, he heard something.

"*Maaark . . .*"

At first he thought he had imagined it. Someone shouting? Mark stood still, pulled off his stocking cap, and held his breath.

"*Maaark . . .*"

No mistake this time. Someone was calling his name.

And Mark was sure of something else. That voice? That was Mr. Maxwell. Yelling his name.

Quick anger surged up in Mark's chest. To be tracked down and caught by Mr. Maxwell! To be led back to the campground, to be dragged off to the blue pickup truck and driven home! To face suspension and all the rest of it!

Mark turned and started running, blindly running, running anywhere, just away. Away from that voice, away from that man.

"*Maaark . . .*"

Rushing fiercely, rushing wildly, Mark pushed through the brush and charged downhill. Jumping over logs and boulders, he slapped the low branches aside as he thrashed forward.

"*Maaark . . .*"

Mark didn't realize how tired he was, but his body knew. He was asking too much of it, pushing too hard and too fast. The slope of the land pulled him forward, demanding split-second decisions. As he jumped down a four-foot drop, Mark expected his legs to absorb the shock of the landing. They refused.

It wasn't a bad fall, but gravity and speed and the weight of the framepack made it a hard one. Mark got his hands up in time to keep from smashing his face on the rocky ground, and he felt a chunk of rock bite into the heel of his left palm.

Mark lay still, sprawled and panting.

Again came the call, or at least a part of it: *"Maa . . ."*

The voice was farther away now, above and behind. Mark only heard half his name. It sounded as if someone had hung up a phone in the middle of a word.

Lying there on the ground, his heart pounding and his injured hand throbbing, Mark had a moment of clarity. His anger and fear were gone, spent. It was as if he was looking down on himself and Mr. Maxwell and the mountain and the campground. The whole scene snapped into focus, and Mark thought, *Why am I running away from him? I was already headed back to the campground, right? So I was going to have to face up to Mr. Maxwell anyway. It might as well be now. I'll just go and find him. Turn myself in. Might even make things easier to do it now instead of later.*

Mark struggled to right himself, wincing as he tried

to push with his left hand. Sitting up, he took a look at it. There was a small cut on the fleshy part of his palm, just below the thumb joint. Not much blood. Mostly a deep bruise from the force of the fall. His right hand hurt too, but it hadn't been cut.

On his feet again, Mark turned to face uphill. He took a deep breath, cupped his hands around this mouth, and yelled. "I'm down here!"

Ten seconds passed, then twenty.

Mark called again, "Hey! I'm down here!"

He waited again, straining to hear, trying to filter out the sound of the wind among the trees.

Nothing.

"Mr. Maxwell? I'm down here!"

Pulling in a deep breath, Mark put all his strength into one more yell: "Mr. Maxwell!"

No reply. Only the wind and the shushing pines and his own deep breaths, now making plumes of vapor in the cold mountain air.

Then Mark remembered. *Mr. Survival—the whistle!* Snatching at the straps and buckles, Mark ripped his pack off and in fifteen seconds had rummaged through the front pockets until he found the little silver coach's whistle that he'd bought at Wal-Mart—an Acme Thunderer. The black lanyard was still rolled up and fastened with a rubber band, just the way it had come out of its package. Mark put the mouthpiece between his lips, sucked in a breath through his nose, and pushed a blast of air through the whistle. The sharp burst of sound left Mark's ears ringing, and even in the wind, he could hear it echo off the ridge high above. Mark strained his ears to hear an answering call. Nothing.

He blew it again and stood still to listen. And again, nothing.

Mark thought, *Maybe Mr. Maxwell was going uphill while I was running down. Maybe he's gone over a ridge up there. Or doubled back toward the main trail. Or maybe the wind and the trees soaked up the sound of my voice—he just didn't hear me call. And now maybe he can hear the whistle, but I can't hear him calling back! That's got to be it! And if he's too far away, then there's only one thing to do: I've got to go up there.*

Mark unrolled the lanyard and hung the whistle around his neck. He was about to lift the pack onto his back and get going, when he remembered something. Digging into another pocket, he pulled out an energy bar, unwrapped it, and forced himself to sit down and eat the whole thing; and then to take a small drink of water. Mark hated the delay, but he knew he was tired, and now he'd have to walk uphill again. He needed the fuel.

Swinging the pack around to his back, he buckled it in place, settled the straps on his shoulders, turned his mind away from the pain of his hand, and set off up the hill, hurrying toward the place where he'd last heard Mr. Maxwell's voice.

He was in such a hurry that for the first time all afternoon, Mark forgot to do something. Something important. He forgot to check his compass.

Nineteen

Here

After about twenty minutes of pushing uphill through the woods, Mark stopped to catch his breath. He figured he must be about where he was when he had first heard Mr. Maxwell call his name.

And again, facing uphill into the wind, he cupped his hands around his mouth and called, "Mr. Maxwell?" And waited. And then he let out a blast from the whistle. And waited.

But again, no answer.

Mark let the whistle drop from his lips. It swung down on its lanyard, and when Mark heard the clink of metal against hard plastic, he glanced down at his chest.

And that's when Mark remembered that he ought to be checking his compass. He lifted it up to eye level and opened the cover. Mark could barely make out the white dot on the red end of the swinging needle. *Time to get out the flashlight*, he thought, and if Mr. Survival had been there, Mark would have given him a hug. Not only did he have a good flashlight, but he had four extra batteries.

The flashlight made it easy to see the compass dial, but Mark didn't like what he saw. Mark thought that since he had been going uphill, he must have been headed north. That's not what the compass reported. The compass told him that he'd been going more west than north. Yes, uphill; but uphill in the wrong direction.

Mark sat down heavily on a boulder to try to figure out what that actually meant. Because when he had heard Mr. Maxwell's first call, he had been headed straight east—back toward the loop trail, the trail he was pretty sure he'd missed. And when he heard that first call, he ran downhill, and he had thought that going downhill meant he was south. But now he saw that he could have run downhill toward the east. Or downhill toward the west. So since he'd just been walking uphill mostly toward the west, was he further west than before? And would the loop trail still be toward the east, or was he too far north now? And which direction would get him close enough so Mr. Maxwell could hear him and answer him?

A gust of cold air found its way down the back of Mark's neck and made him shiver. He had been expecting the wind to die down after sunset like it usually did. Not tonight. It was still blowing strong out of the north. If anything, it was picking up a little.

Mark turned off the flashlight, and then immediately turned it back on. The bright light had ruined his night vision, and now he needed it on to see anything. And he didn't mind. He liked having it on. It gave him a little island of light in the gathering darkness.

Staring at the compass face again, he forced himself to think, forced himself to push back the rising fears. *So I know the loop trail is to the east. I know it is. I know that. And the loop trail goes all the way up to the high ridge. And I know I'm not that far up on the mountain. I know that. So if I go east, and if I'm careful, then I have to find the trail. I have to.*

Mark looked at his compass again and then started walking. It was slow going. He had to keep the flashlight on to keep from banging into branches or tripping over rocks and roots. He held the flashlight in his right hand because his left one still hurt from the fall. Mark kept count, and after every thirty steps he stopped to check the compass again. Working his way due east across the shoulder of the mountain took all his concentration.

The next thirty minutes seemed like six hours to Mark. As he stopped to check his direction again, he noticed that the wind had slowed down a bit and shifted direction as well. According to the compass, the wind was now coming from the east.

Mark shined his flashlight upward. He saw the swaying maple and birch branches overhead, saw the frosty vapor from his breath, visible for only a second before the wind snatched it away. He turned off the light to see if there were any stars. He forced himself to leave the light off long enough for his eyes to adjust to the darkness a little. No stars. No moon. Only the wind and the trees and the mountain and the night.

Pulling in a huge breath, Mark yelled: "Mr. Maxwell!"

Mark hardly recognized the echo from a rock face somewhere above him: "Mr. Maxwell!" The voice of the echo sounded like a very small boy, scared and alone.

Mark turned on his flashlight and kept walking due east.

As Mark pushed ahead, complete darkness and a bone-chilling cold settled over the mountain. Another kind of darkness crept into Mark's mind. Grimly, Mark thought, *It's not going to happen. I'm not going to find Mr. Maxwell. He's not even up here anymore. He's back down at the cabins, sipping coffee and talking with the park rangers about how to rescue the stupid kid who got himself . . . lost.*

For a kid alone in the woods, lost is a bad word, especially after dark. So Mark avoided it. He tried to keep the word out of his mind. But finally, after another twenty minutes of walking and calling and hearing nothing but his own voice, Mark couldn't help himself.

I'm lost, he thought. *I mean, I'm not really lost, because I've got a map and I've got a compass, and I know that sooner or later I can find my way back to the Barker Falls Trail. I'm sure I can do that. Except it won't be easy, not in the dark. Or when I'm this tired. Right now, tonight, I'm not gonna be going down to the campground, or anywhere near it. So for tonight, I'm lost . . . but not really. I'm just . . . here.*

Twenty

Camp

Mark was glad that he'd spent that night sleeping out in the barn back in February. That had been good practice. Not at camping out, but at being alone. Because being alone was the hard part.

Standing in the woods, Mark held his flashlight at arm's length and began to turn slowly, letting the beam sweep a twenty- or thirty-foot circle around him. He was looking for a campsite.

Mark knew he wasn't going to find a big open space like the one where he and Leon had slept that night. And really, he didn't want an open place. Mark wanted shelter.

Uphill from where he was standing, he caught a glimpse of a large rock beyond a thicket of hemlock and birch trees. The stone looked almost white in the beam of his flashlight.

Walking closer for a better look, Mark saw it was more than a rock. It was the downhill face of a granite outcropping. The vertical face of the outcropping rose up about thirty feet to the top ledge, which then sloped back to gradually rejoin the mountainside. Going around to the left side of the formation, Mark found a place in close to the rock where the ground was nearly level. There were some low bushes and a scattering of small rocks, but the ground was basically clear. Since it was the west side of the rock, he was well out of the wind. Best of all, six or eight feet above the level area, the rock jutted outward three or four feet. It certainly wasn't a roof, but at that moment the whole setup looked perfect to Mark. He unsnapped and unbuckled his framepack and let it drop to the ground. He was home.

First thing, Mark dug into the front pouch of his pack and found another energy bar. It was gone in less than two minutes. Then he had a small drink of water, and he was ready to get to work.

Mark's hands were cold, and having to constantly hold the metal flashlight didn't help. So he quickly found his other light, the headlamp. He had to loosen the headband a little so it would fit over his stocking cap, and in the process discovered that his fingers were so cold they were clumsy. But he got the job done, and then out loud he said, "Must be twenty-five up here! Wish I'd brought some gloves!"

But Mark did have plenty of extra socks in his pack, so a minute later he was wearing a pair on his hands like mittens, pleased with his inventiveness.

The headlamp worked great. Even with the thing set on medium power, Mark felt like he had a searchlight mounted on his forehead. He wished he had put it on earlier. Wherever he looked the light was there instantly, with no effort, no thought process, and it left both his hands free.

With his sock-mittens as hand protectors, Mark pulled up the few leafless bushes that were in the way. He started to pick up and toss some rocks out of the way, then stopped. Taking a flat rock by one edge, he got down on his knees and used it to scrape away all the pine needles and leaves and brush from an area about ten feet in all directions. *I know I'm not supposed to make a fire without a grown-up around*, he thought, *but this is an emergency, right? And it's not like I have matches or a lighter, so I might not even be able to get one started. But it's cold, and I'm out here alone, so I'm gonna try!*

Mark soon had the area cleared and had dug out a fire pit and lined it with rocks. It was about four feet from where he planned to put his sleeping bag, because he wanted to sleep with his back against the rock wall. *That's my house*, he thought, *and this is my front yard.*

Gathering some deadwood was easy, and he broke

the thicker branches into small logs, cracking them over a rock the way Leon had taught him. His left hand kept hurting, but not enough to hinder his work. In ten minutes he had four neat piles of wood laid out next to the fire pit, sorted by size, from tiny twigs to small logs.

Next he found a dead birch tree and peeled off some strips of bark. Squatting down by his fire pit, Mark pulled off his mittens and began separating the birch bark into the thinnest possible layers, some of them even thinner than paper, almost transparent. Then, using his fingernails, he tore the thin pieces into narrow strips, and finally rolled the shredded bark between his palms. He kept at it until he had four loose wads of birch bark tinder, each a little smaller than a golf ball.

From the zipper pocket of his pack he pulled out the magnesium block with the striker bar attached along one edge. From a different pocket he took out the four-inch-long piece of hacksaw blade. Mark placed a wad of the bark on a flat rock in the center of his fire pit. He put the end of the striker bar directly onto the shredded birch bark. Then, with a quick motion that looked like he was peeling a carrot, Mark struck the hacksaw blade against the striker bar.

A bright flash of sparks sprayed downward at the birch tinder. Their brilliance practically blinded him, but Mark blinked away the blue spots before his eyes and struck again, and then again. The sparks flew thick and hot, and on the sixth or seventh strike, the birch bark sputtered, then caught fire! Quickly adding another clump of tinder to the little blaze, Mark fed it twigs, one at a time, until the fire was burning well enough to accept a couple of the smaller logs.

It was his very own campfire, his first, and Mark would have liked to sit there in the cheerful warmth of it all night long, glowing with pride. But he couldn't, at least not just yet. He had other work to do.

At first Mark didn't know where he was. And he didn't know what was making that sound. Then his memory flooded full. He knew where he was, but he still wasn't sure about the sound. He snaked a hand up out his sleeping bag to reach for his flashlight.

It was the space blanket, rustling and crinkling in the breeze. When his campfire had died down to embers, Mark had spread the plastic blanket over his sleeping bag and pack to keep off the morning frost. He had put small rocks along the edges to hold the covering in place, but one corner of the blanket must have pulled loose as he slept.

Mark didn't want to move. He had been warm and perfectly comfortable. And Mark especially didn't want to be awake, because that meant he'd have to get back to sleep, and it had been hard enough the first time. But now that he was awake, he had to move. He had no choice. He needed to use the bathroom.

The bright flashlight hurt his eyes, so he shut them tight. Then he peeked at his watch. Three thirty. Sitting up in his sleeping bag, Mark shone the light around his campsite. Not much to see. A few pieces of leftover wood next to the fire pit, his jacket and boots there beside him, his yellow frame pack next to his sleeping bag, and where he'd been lying down, a sweatshirt he'd folded up to use for a pillow.

And within easy reach, a sturdy piece of maple branch, about five feet long. It was a club. In case of a bear. A black bear. The kind Mark had read about. The kind of bear that stood three feet tall at the shoulder, and stretched six feet from nose to tail. The kind that had four massive paws with three-inch-long claws on each one. The kind that could run thirty miles an hour and climb right up a tree. The kind that lived in the mountains of New Hampshire. That kind of bear.

Which was the main reason Mark had had trouble getting to sleep.

And thinking of bears, Mark shined his flashlight beam out into the woods. He was looking for his yellow stuff sack. After eating a Snickers bar for dinner, he had put his five remaining candy bars and four remaining energy bars into the bag, along with his soap and toothpaste. Then he had used his dental floss to hang the sack from a pine branch. It was fifteen or twenty feet in the air, and it was a good distance from where he planned to sleep. Because that's what Mr.

Survival had said you should do with things that smell nice or taste good when you're out in bear country.

Out as far as his flashlight would shine, Mark could just barely see the outline of his bright yellow stuff sack, swinging in the wind. *No bears*, he thought. Then he added, *Yet*.

The ice crystals from where he'd breathed on his sleeping bag flaked off in a tiny shower of glitter as Mark squirmed out, slipped into his freezing cold boots, and then walked twenty feet away from his campsite.

A minute later he hurried back toward the warmth of his sleeping bag. He was about to take off his boots. And stopped.

A sound. It was close, coming from uphill. Coming his way. And not quietly now. Something heavy, snapping sticks as it came forward.

Mark dropped his flashlight and grabbed for his club.

And then out of the darkness, a voice called to him, hoarse and rough.

"Mark—it's okay. It's me. I need . . . help."

Twenty-one

Found

"Mr. Maxwell?!"

Mark grabbed his flashlight and trotted toward the voice. "Mr. Maxwell . . . where were you? I tried . . . I tried to . . ." And then Mark saw him.

Mr. Maxwell squinted and turned his face from the glare of the flashlight. Visibly shivering, his hat was gone. His hair was matted down, wet with sweat, with steam rising off his head into the freezing air. His face was pale as a full moon and twisted by pain, his lips purple.

"It's my . . . ankle," he said, grunting as he took another step. His voice wasn't much louder than a dry whisper.

Mark aimed his light down at Mr. Maxwell's boots, and then trained the beam on the right one. A black leather belt had been wrapped five or six times around the outside of the tan hunting boot and buckled tightly into place. The pant leg above the boot top had been partly torn away and Mark could see scrapes and a deep bruise on the exposed skin.

Moving quickly to his side, Mark grabbed his right arm, said, "Hold on," and then helped Mr. Maxwell walk the last ten yards.

At the side of the outcropping, Mark said, "Sit here."

With Mark's help Mr. Maxwell eased himself down slowly until he was sitting on the ground, his back against the rock. Ten seconds later Mark said, "Lean forward," and when Mr. Maxwell did, Mark wrapped the space blanket around his back and over his shoulders. Then Mark unzipped his sleeping bag and tucked it around him like a blanket, pulling it down to cover his legs as well.

Taking off his stocking cap, Mark pulled it onto Mr. Maxwell's head. It was too small to go all the way over his ears. Mark said, "A person loses most of his body heat from his head. You said that in class, remember?"

Mr. Maxwell smiled weakly and nodded. "Right."

Mark pulled on his jacket and his headlamp, walked over to some fallen trees and quickly gathered an armload of sticks. Then he looked around the edge of his fire pit until he found the two wads of birch tinder he hadn't used earlier. Using a stick, he stirred the ashes of his campfire to see if there might be a live ember hiding there. Nothing.

So Mark pushed the warm ashes to one side, laid the tinder in the center, pulled the striker bar and the hacksaw blade from his jacket pocket and in thirty seconds had a fire kindled. Twigs, then sticks, then small branches, and then a couple of larger sticks. An occasional gust of wind blew the smoke back toward Mr. Maxwell, but mostly the fire pit was well shielded by the outcropping.

Glancing at Mr. Maxwell in the firelight, Mark was scared. He looked awful. "Hey," he said, "you must be thirsty!"

Mr. Maxwell nodded, so Mark grabbed the unopened liter bottle from his pack. "Here. But make it last, okay? I've only got a little more in the other bottle. But I've got some food. Back in a minute."

Mr. Maxwell watched the headlight bob through the darkness as Mark trotted out to his hanging stuff sack, saw him lower it to the ground and then trot back.

He fished into the sack, then holding out one of each, Mark said, "Energy bar or Snickers?"

Mr. Maxwell said, "Energy, please." The water must have helped, because his voice sounded more normal.

Unwrapping the bar for him, Mark said, "Okay. But eat slowly. Because if you chew it smaller, it gets absorbed faster, right?"

His mouth already full, Mr. Maxwell nodded. The

bar was gone in less than a minute, so Mark said, "Better have a Snickers, too. I have five of them."

Mr. Maxwell didn't refuse.

Mark broke up some thicker dead branches, and soon the warmth of the fire was helping to cut the chill. Some color had returned to Mr. Maxwell's cheeks. He looked a little more like a science teacher and a little less like a ghost.

Mark said, "Is your ankle real bad?"

Mr. Maxwell tried to smile. "Well, it's not good. I'm pretty sure it's broken. Didn't unlace my boot to look."

"How did it happen?"

"Me being stupid, that's how," said Mr. Maxwell. "I tracked you to the place on the loop trail where it goes up to the ridge. Then I saw you went straight. So I figured you were taking a short cut across, and I wanted to get to the trail before you did. So I didn't track you. I went across above you on the mountain, because I was afraid that if I got too close, you'd hear me and hide or run off and really get yourself lost out there. So I got to the trail, and I figured I was above you, so I started hurrying down. Which is two mistakes at once—hurrying when I was alone, and hurrying downhill. I knew I was tired and dehydrated, and the light was getting bad, but I hurried anyway. Just a lot of stupid stuff all at once. And all it took was one stretch of steep trail, and one rock that wasn't steady, and one big fat boot coming down too fast and too sloppy. The rock tipped and I went down hard. My foot got wedged, and then another rock fell in on top, a big one. That's the one that hurt me. I couldn't lift it off. And I called out your name four or five times, and then I guess I passed out for a while. It hurt pretty bad."

"You didn't hear me call back?" asked Mark. "Because I heard you yell. At first I ran away, downhill. And I'm sorry about that. But then I called back. I even blew my whistle and went back uphill looking for you. But I figured you must have headed back down to the camp. I walked east so I could get back to the main trail. That's how I ended up here."

Mr. Maxwell said, "I did hear the whistle. And I yelled my head off, but my throat was too dry and my voice didn't last long. You must have been downwind of me and too far away." Mr. Maxwell shook his head and made a wry face. "Besides, I figured maybe you heard me, and then lit out to get as far away from me as you could."

There was an awkward silence. Mark got up and put two more pieces of wood on the fire. Then he asked, "So how'd you get your foot loose?"

"Pure dumb luck," said Mr. Maxwell, "that's how. It was almost dark, and I was in a lot of pain. But right there, right next to the trail, there were some young maple trees. And I looked at the rock pinning my ankle, and I could see that if I had a lever, I could pry it up enough to get my foot out."

"But deadwood breaks too easily," said Mark. "I've been breaking up maple all night for firewood."

"Who said anything about deadwood?" asked Mr. Maxwell. "I used a live maple, about eight feet long."

"You broke off a live tree?"

"Nope," said Mr. Maxwell. "Didn't break it. Cut it. With this."

Mr. Maxwell stuck his hand out from under the sleeping bag. He was holding the tool. The knife.

"Oh," said Mark. He felt his face turning red.

"Here," said Mr. Maxwell, tossing it to Mark, "open up the saw."

"The saw?" said Mark. "Sure. The saw."

Mark turned the tool over in his hands a couple times, then pulled at one of the blades. It was a file. "Oops," he said, pushing it back into the handle. "I always get the file and the saw mixed up." Mark fiddled some more and then pulled out a blunt, serrated knife blade. On the third try he found the saw and pulled it out until it clicked all the way open.

"That's a great little saw," said Mr. Maxwell. "Ripped through four inches of green maple tree in about fifteen minutes. Then I knocked off the branches, lopped off the top, got a smaller rock to use for a fulcrum, and zip, got myself free in three minutes flat. Nothing like a simple machine. And then later, I smelled wood smoke and started working my way toward it. Figured it had to be you." Nodding at the tool, Mr. Maxwell said, "Better close that up."

"Sure," said Mark. He pushed at the back of the saw blade. It wouldn't move. "Guess it's stuck."

"You have to unlock it," Mr. Maxwell said.

"Right," said Mark, but he didn't know where to push to make the blade close.

After he'd fiddled with it for about ten seconds, Mr. Maxwell said, "Here." He held out his hand and Mark gave him the tool. With a simple motion of his thumb, Mr. Maxwell pushed down the lock catch and snapped the saw blade shut.

Mr. Maxwell looked at Mark in the orange firelight, and quietly he said, "Mark, I know it's not your knife. It's got Jason's name scratched on the handle. I went to my truck to tell you I knew, but you weren't there. I wanted to tell you that I understood why you took the blame that way. But you weren't there. And I'm not mad at you for running off. You should have told me the truth, that it was Jason's knife, but I understand why you didn't. I've been pretty nasty. And I'm sorry. This is all my fault. All of it. I'm going to make sure you don't get in trouble. None at all. And I hope you can forgive me."

Mark's chest felt so tight he could hardly breathe.

Mr. Maxwell said, "And you don't have to say anything. Better if you don't. So that's that."

After the silence had stretched to twenty or thirty seconds Mr. Maxwell said, "Say, do you think I could have another Snickers bar? I'm still pretty hungry."

"Sure!" Mark jumped up and got him one.

Talking with his mouth full, Mr. Maxwell said, "So how come you got onto the loop trail in the first place?"

"Well, you see . . . I wanted to get back to the campground before dark. I guessed everyone would think I was lost. But I'm not, because I've got my compass and Mrs. Farr gave us all a map. But if everyone *thought* I was lost, then it would turn into a big deal. And that would ruin the whole week for everybody. And I didn't want that."

Mr. Maxwell didn't try to talk. It would have been hard for him at that moment. And not just because his mouth was full of candy bar.

He'd had this feeling many times during his life as a teacher. Only not so much recently. This feeling of quiet awe at the basic decency of people. And especially children, how they understand about right and wrong. He'd seen it so many times, and then he would forget about it. About how if people are given half a chance, they do the right thing. Sitting there with his ankle throbbing, Mr. Maxwell felt certain he wouldn't forget it again. He was glad for the swirling wood smoke. It gave him a good reason to let his eyes water a little.

When he'd finished the Snickers, Mr. Maxwell saw the piece of maple branch on the ground beside Mark's sleeping area. He reached out from under the sleeping bag and picked it up. "What's this, Mark?"

Mark said, "That's my bear stick."

"Oh," said Mr. Maxwell. "Right. It's a nice one. Good and sturdy. Mind if I borrow it?"

Mark looked surprised, but he said, "No . . . you can use it."

"Good," said Mr. Maxwell, "because it looks like a good cane to me." He tossed the sleeping bag to one side and struggled to his feet. "I know you've got a couple of flashlights. You say you've got a map and a compass?"

"Right here," said Mark, patting his jacket pocket.

"Great," said Mr. Maxwell. "Then let's get this fire put out and break camp. If we go due east anywhere below Barker Falls, we'll run smack into the main trail. Can't miss it. I'm guessing it's about maybe an hour from here—at my speed, that is. We get to the trail and head down, and by sunup, we'll be almost back at the campground. Probably make it in time for breakfast. First morning it's always pancakes. Ready to go?"

Mark was ready.

Twenty-two

Home

Mr. Maxwell had to stop every fifteen minutes or so and rest. He didn't complain once as he limped along, but Mark could tell by the way Mr. Maxwell breathed that each step was painful. It ended up taking them almost four hours to hike down to the campground.

By the time they arrived breakfast was over, but the kitchen crew was happy to fire up the griddle and make a special batch of pancakes for the returning adventurers.

The ranger came in as Mark and Mr. Maxwell were having seconds. "Bill! Am I glad to see you!" Reaching out to shake a hand that was sticky with maple syrup, he said, "And you must be Mark Chelmsley. Gave us all a scare there for a while. Glad you're both back safe and sound."

Mr. Maxwell wiped off his chin. He winked at

Mark and said, "Jim, this boy and I were a little disappointed that you didn't have a big posse all set to come rescue us. We thought there'd be dogs and helicopters and state police all over the place this morning. It's almost like you didn't care."

The ranger smiled. "When Mrs. Leghorn came and told me what you told her to, well, as far as I was concerned that was the end of it. She said you'd found the boy and that you'd bring him back soon. So you know what I did? I sat down and read the paper for a while, then I went home, ate a nice dinner with my wife, watched some baseball on TV, and went to bed. And look, you're back—soon, just like you said! Now, I won't say that we weren't all a little concerned. Especially early this morning. Mrs. Leghorn came and told me that we had to call the whole program off and get the National Guard in here. But I told her that we'd wait and see till about noon. So really, you two got home about three hours early!" Looking down at Mr. Maxwell's right leg, he said, "What happened? Bear getcha?"

Mr. Maxwell smiled and shook his head. "Nope. A rock."

The ranger said, "Well, if you need someone to drive you over to the clinic in Bushelton, let me know." Then looking at Mark he said, "I'm mighty glad old Bill found you, young fella."

Mr. Maxwell shook his head. "It didn't happen that way, Jim. We found each other."

Ten minutes later the boy and his teacher stood outside the door of the main lodge. Mr. Maxwell said, "I've got to go get this ankle looked at. Think you can find your way back to the Raven's Nest without getting lost?"

Mark grinned. "Can do."

"Okay then. See you later." Mr. Maxwell turned and took a step, then quickly turned back. "Oh—almost forgot." He reached into his pocket and took out the knife. Holding it up he said, "Tell Jason that I'll keep this for him until the end of the week, okay? And tell him that I'm going to have a little talk with him. About obeying rules."

Mark said, "I'll tell him. Thanks, Mr. Maxwell."

And Mr. Maxwell smiled and said, "Thank *you*, Mark."

When the orange buses rocked to a halt in the school driveway late Friday afternoon, a friendly mob of grown-ups was waiting. Every child stepped down into a cheerful flurry of hugs and hellos. Even some of the boys who thought they didn't want to be hugged and kissed put up with it. It had only been a week, but it had seemed much longer.

"Mark! Over here!"

Mark turned and saw Leon waving at him. Then Anya got out of the car and started waving too. Mark ran down the driveway and gave them each a hug.

Anya kissed him on the cheek. "It is too quiet with only Leon around the house! I am so glad you are home."

"Me, too!" said Mark.

As Leon put the framepack into the trunk, he asked, "You had a good time?"

"It was great! We did some hiking, and we stayed up late one night and looked at the stars through telescopes. And I saw an eagle and some bear tracks—it was great!"

Mark got in the backseat, and while they waited for the cars ahead of them to move, he leaned forward and kept talking. "Yeah, and on the third day the guys in my cabin got to help the ranger check for missing trail markers, and he said that we . . ."

There was a knock on Leon's window. Leon lowered it, and Mr. Maxwell said, "Mr. Lermentov? I'm Bill Maxwell, Mark's science teacher. We talked for a couple minutes on Monday afternoon, and I wanted to let you know I was sorry if my call worried you. I know the ranger called a little later to explain the situation, but I wanted to thank you myself for being so understanding."

Leon shook the hand that Mr. Maxwell offered, and said, "Of course, Mr. Maxwell. This is my wife, Anya. We are glad to meet you. We have heard of you often from Mark. And he's just telling us how he had such good fun."

Mr. Maxwell smiled broadly and said, "Best week ever." Then bending down so he could look into the backseat, he said. "Mark, this is for you."

And Mr. Maxwell handed him the knife in its leather sheath.

Mark looked confused. "But . . . Jason . . . "

Mr. Maxwell shook his head. "Jason wouldn't take it. He said it was yours now. So I guess it is. Well, I've got to run. Nice to meet you folks."

And with that Mr. Maxwell turned and went back toward the buses, the cast on his right foot making him sway from side to side as he walked.

Mark lowered his window and leaned out. "Mr. Maxwell?" he called.

Mr. Maxwell stopped and turned around.

"I . . . I'll see you on Monday."

Mr. Maxwell smiled and nodded. "You bet, Mark. See you Monday."

As Anya opened the door from the garage to the kitchen, the phone was ringing. She answered it and then called, "Mark . . . it's for you. It's your father."

"Hello?"

"Mark! Good to hear your voice, Son. We knew you'd be getting home about now. Heard from Anya about that business on your camping trip. Everything work out all right?"

"Yup," said Mark. "It all worked out fine."

His mom joined the conversation, and she said, "But you *were* lost on a mountain all night? All by yourself? Is that right?"

"Not all night," said Mark, "and I wasn't really lost. I had a compass and everything. It was just too hard to hike in the dark. And I got tired, too. I'll tell you the whole story when you get home."

"That'll be sooner than you think," said his dad. "Your mom got worried, so we hopped on the Concorde this morning and flew into New York three hours ago."

"You were worried too, Robert!" said his mother.

"Sure, I was worried too. I admit it. So anyway, Mark, we're going to spend the night here in Scarsdale and drive up tomorrow. Be there about lunchtime."

"Great!" said Mark. "Because . . . I want to talk about something . . . with both of you."

"You bet," said his dad. "We'll talk, we'll do a little hiking, maybe drive up to Hanover—it'll be a great weekend."

"Talk about what?" said his mom, and Mark could hear the concern in her voice.

Mark hesitated, then took a deep breath and said, "I want to talk about maybe staying here. Like going to school in Whitson next year. Because they've got a good accelerated program at the middle school—my friend Jason says so. And Jason's big brother? He went to school here, and he just got accepted into Princeton, so the schools aren't bad, they couldn't be. And . . . and that's what I want to talk about."

There was a long silence on the line. His mom spoke first.

"Well . . . I thought we had this all worked out Mark, about next year and Runyon Academy? And really, I think that . . ."

His dad broke in, "Mark? Absolutely. If you want to talk about it, we'll talk. That whole Runyon thing? That's not written in stone. So tomorrow you and your mom and me, we'll all sit down and talk about it. That sound right to you, Lo?"

Mark heard the tiniest hesitation, but his mom said, "Of course . . . Yes. We'll talk about it. Because all we want is what's best for you, Mark. That's all we want."

The conversation seemed to have hit a stone wall.

Then Mark's dad said, "I was putting a coat in the closet here Mark, and I saw some of your stuff—your lacrosse stick and some soccer balls—sports stuff, mostly. You want me to toss anything in the car before we come tomorrow?"

"Yeah, that'd be great. Bring the stick and both of the balls, and my soccer shoes, too. I think they'll still fit."

Mark's mom said, "Mark? I'll hang up now. See you tomorrow. I love you, dear."

"Love you, too, Mom."

After the click his dad said, "So, anything else I should bring?"

"Can't think of anything . . ." said Mark. Then, "Wait. . . where are you now, Dad?"

"In my office on the second floor."

"Could you go down the hall to my old bedroom?" asked Mark.

"Sure. Hold on a sec."

Mark heard the casters of the desk chair, then footsteps, and he could picture his dad going out of his doorway, then turning left and walking beside the curving banister to the third door on the left, Mark's old room.

"Here I am, Mark, but there's nothing here, remember? You cleaned the place out."

"Okay," said Mark, "now go over to the radiator by the window."

"The radiator? What for?" asked his dad.

"Are you there?" said Mark.

"Yup. Listen. . . ." And Mark heard a clank as his dad tapped the phone against the metal.

"Good," said Mark. "Now, tip the radiator back toward the wall a little, and look under the right front leg. . . . Do you see it?"

"Wait . . ." said his dad. Mark heard a soft grunt of effort, and then, "A *penny*? You're having me do all this for a penny?"

"Do you have it?" asked Mark.

"Yes, I've got it," said his dad.

"Great. You can bring it with you tomorrow, okay, Dad? And don't get it mixed up with your other change, okay? I want *that* penny."

"I get it," said his dad. "This is a lucky penny, right?"

Mark said, "Yeah . . . sort of."

"Haven't I always told you there's no such thing as luck?" and as he said that, Mark could picture the look on his dad's face.

"I know that," said Mark. "It's . . . it's just a penny, Dad. I left it there when we moved, and now I want to have it up here in New Hampshire. That's all."

A quick moment passed, and his dad said, "Sure. I understand, Mark. I'll keep this safe for you."

"Thanks."

"No problem." His dad was quiet for a second or two, and then he said, "So, I'll see you tomorrow, okay?"

"Okay, Dad."

And then his dad said, "I'm proud of you, Son."

His dad had said those words to him before, probably dozens of times. But as Mark heard them this time, the words sounded different, and they felt different. Everything felt different.

Mark drew in a deep breath, and he swallowed hard, and he blinked his eyes a few times. Then he smiled and said, "Thanks, Dad. See you tomorrow."

WHAT'S NEXT FROM THE MASTER OF
THE SCHOOL STORY?

Turn the page for an excerpt from Andrew
Clements's new hardcover novel,

THE
REPORT
CARD

Coming soon from Simon & Schuster Books for Young Readers

one

BAD GRADES

There were only about fifteen kids on the late bus because it was Friday afternoon. I sat near the back with Stephen, and he kept pestering me.

"Come on, Nora. I showed you my report card. I want to see if I beat you in math. Let me see what you got. Come on."

"No," I said. "No means no. I'm not opening it. I had to go to school every day, and I had to sit there and take the tests and quizzes when they told me to. But I have a choice about when I look at my grades, and right now I choose not to. So ask me on Monday."

Stephen is my best friend, but I'm not sure he would have admitted it. If any of his buddies had been on the bus, he wouldn't have been sitting anywhere near me. In fifth grade a guy's best friend isn't supposed to be a girl— which is one of the most immature ideas in the universe. Your best friend is the person you care about the most and who cares back just as much. And that's the way it was with me and Stephen. It wasn't a girl-boy thing. It was just a fact.

Stephen was persistent. He'd been having a hard time with his schoolwork for the past ten weeks, and he was obsessed with grades. So he wouldn't shut up about my report card. On and on and on. And our bus ride home took twenty minutes. "Come on, Nora. It's not fair. You know what I got, but I don't know what you got. I wanna see your grades. C'mon, lemme see 'em."

Another fact: Sometimes no doesn't mean no forever. There was only about a block to go before our bus stop, but I couldn't stand Stephen's whining another second. Besides, the truth is, I was dying to know my spelling grade. I was sure about my grades in all the other subjects, but I thought I might have messed up in spelling. So I pulled my report card out of my backpack and slapped it into Stephen's hands. I didn't even care that my whole name was printed right on the label: Nora Rose Rowley.

"Here," I said. "This is your prize for being the most annoying person in the world."

Stephen said, "All riiight!" and he had those grades out of the envelope in about three seconds.

Stephen's face went blank and his mouth dropped open. And it was like he couldn't talk. Or breathe. He finally spluttered and said, "No *way*, Nora! This *can't* be right! Mrs. Noyes . . . and Mrs. Zhang . . . and *everybody*! These are the wrong grades!"

I ignored his amazement. I said, "Just tell me what I got in spelling, okay?"

Stephen's eyes flickered down the page and then he said, "You . . . you got a C."

"*Rats*!" and I kicked the seat in front of us. "I *knew* it! A lousy C—how could I be so *stupid*!"

Stephen was wishing he hadn't begged to see my grades, and his face showed it. He gulped and said, "Um . . . Nora? I hate to tell you, but all your other grades are . . ."

I cut him off. "I know what they are."

Stephen was completely confused. He said, "But . . . but if you know what the others are, then why are you mad about the C in spelling? Because all the others are . . . *Ds*! You got a D in *everything*! All Ds—except for that one C."

"*Rats*!" I said again. "*Spelling*!"

Stephen struggled on. "But . . . but spelling is your *best* grade," and to reassure himself he said, ". . . because a C is *better* than a D, right?"

I shook my head, and then I said more than I should have. "Not always," I said. "C is *not* better if you're trying to get a D."

That *really* confused Stephen. And I didn't want him to have time to think about it. I grabbed my report card back and said, "So what did you get in spelling?"

I knew the answer to that question because I'd already seen Stephen's report card. Plus, spelling is always his best subject.

Stephen said, "I . . . I got an A."

"And is that the grade you were trying to get?"

He squinted and then said, "Um . . . yeah, I guess so."

"Then you got what you were trying for, and that's good. That's a good grade, Stephen."

He said, "Um . . . thanks."

We got off the bus at the corner and started walking along the street toward our houses. Stephen didn't say another word.

I could tell he was worried about my grades. And that was just like him—to be worried about someone other than himself. Which is why it was a good thing that Stephen had someone like me looking out for him.

Because I had gotten those Ds on purpose. I had meant to get *all* Ds. And those Ds were probably going to get me into big trouble.

But I didn't care about that.

I had gotten those Ds for Stephen.